RUDOLPH THE RED-NOSED REINDEER®

THE ISLAND OF MISFIT TOYS™

RUDOLPH THE RED-NOSED REINDEER®

THE ISLAND OF MISFIT TOYS™

WRITTEN BY
Brendan Deneen

ILLUSTRATED BY
George Kambadais

COLORED BY
Jordi Escuin

LETTERED BY
David C. Hopkins

SQUARE
FISH

An
Imprint
of Macmillan
175 Fifth Avenue
New York, NY 10010
mackids.com

RUDOLPH
THE RED-NOSED REINDEER®:
THE ISLAND OF MISFIT TOYS™.
Written by Brendan Deneen
in association with Ardden Entertainment.
Rudolph the Red-Nosed Reindeer
© & ® or TM The Rudolph Co., L.P.
All elements under license to Character Arts, LLC.
All rights reserved. Printed in the United States of America by
Worzalla, Stevens Point, Wisconsin.

Square Fish books may be purchased for business or promotional use.
For information on bulk purchases, please contact the Macmillan Corporate
and Premium Sales Department at (800) 221-7945 x5442
or by e-mail at specialmarkets@macmillan.com.

Library of Congress Cataloging-in-Publication Data Available
ISBN 978-1-250-05063-2 • First Square Fish Edition: 2014

Book designed
by Anna Booth
Square Fish
logo designed
by Filomena Tuosto

10 9 8 7 6 5 4 3 2 1

For Eloise and Charlotte, the best gifts I've ever received.
—B.D.

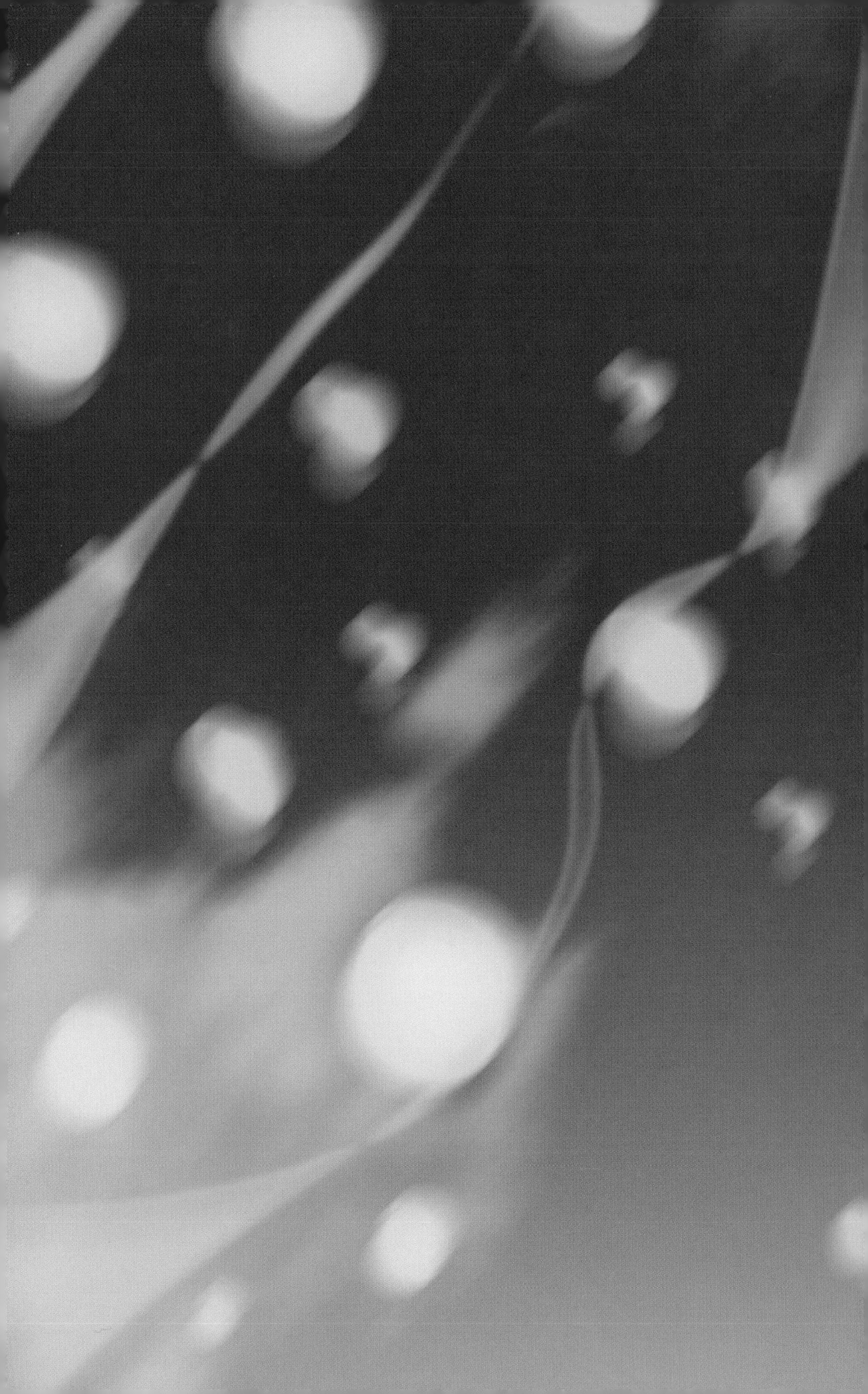

RUDOLPH THE RED-NOSED REINDEER®

THE ISLAND OF MISFIT TOYS

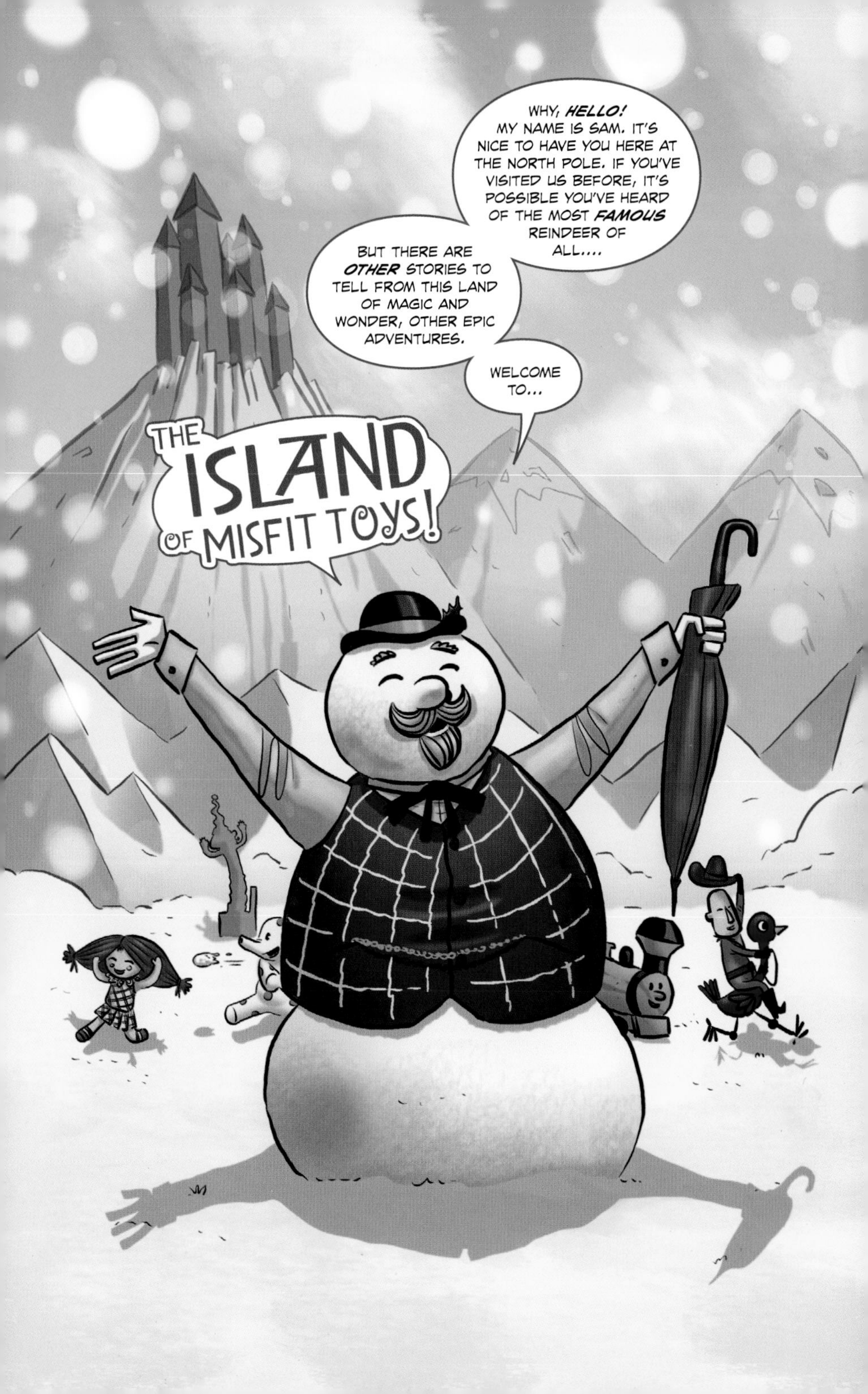
WHY, *HELLO!* MY NAME IS SAM. IT'S NICE TO HAVE YOU HERE AT THE NORTH POLE. IF YOU'VE VISITED US BEFORE, IT'S POSSIBLE YOU'VE HEARD OF THE MOST *FAMOUS* REINDEER OF ALL....
BUT THERE ARE *OTHER* STORIES TO TELL FROM THIS LAND OF MAGIC AND WONDER, OTHER EPIC ADVENTURES.
WELCOME TO...
THE ISLAND OF MISFIT TOYS!

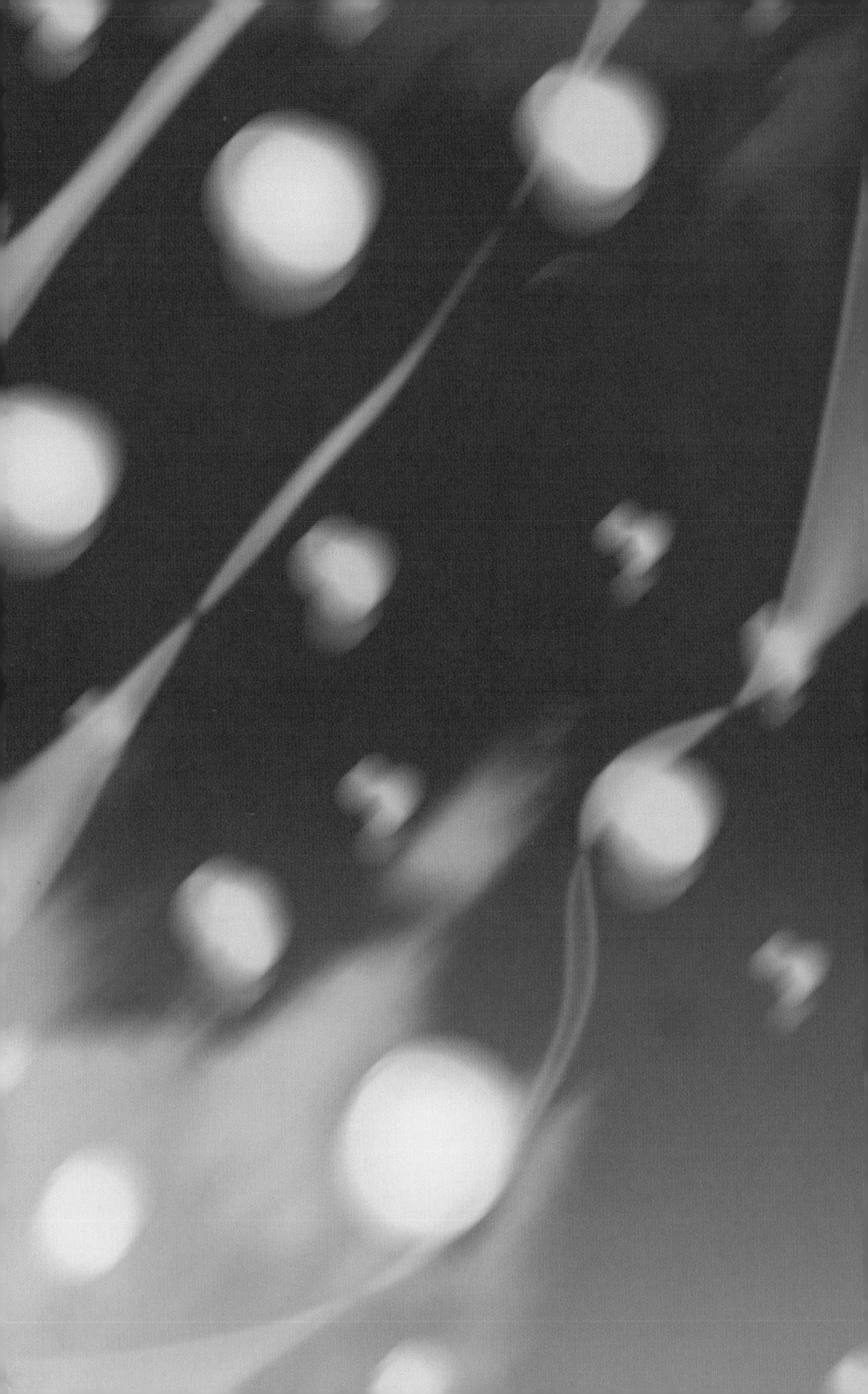

CHAPTER ONE

THE STORM

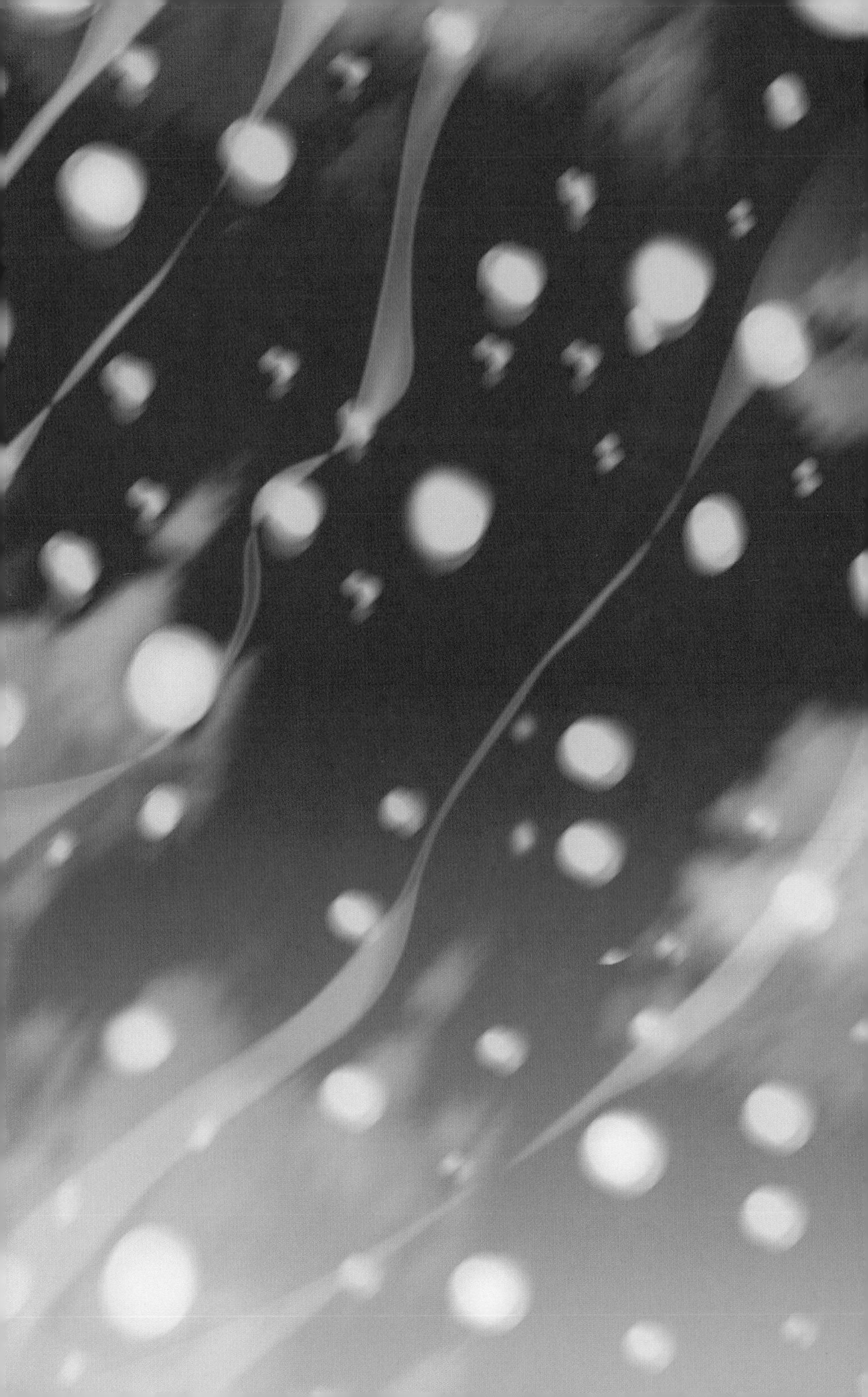

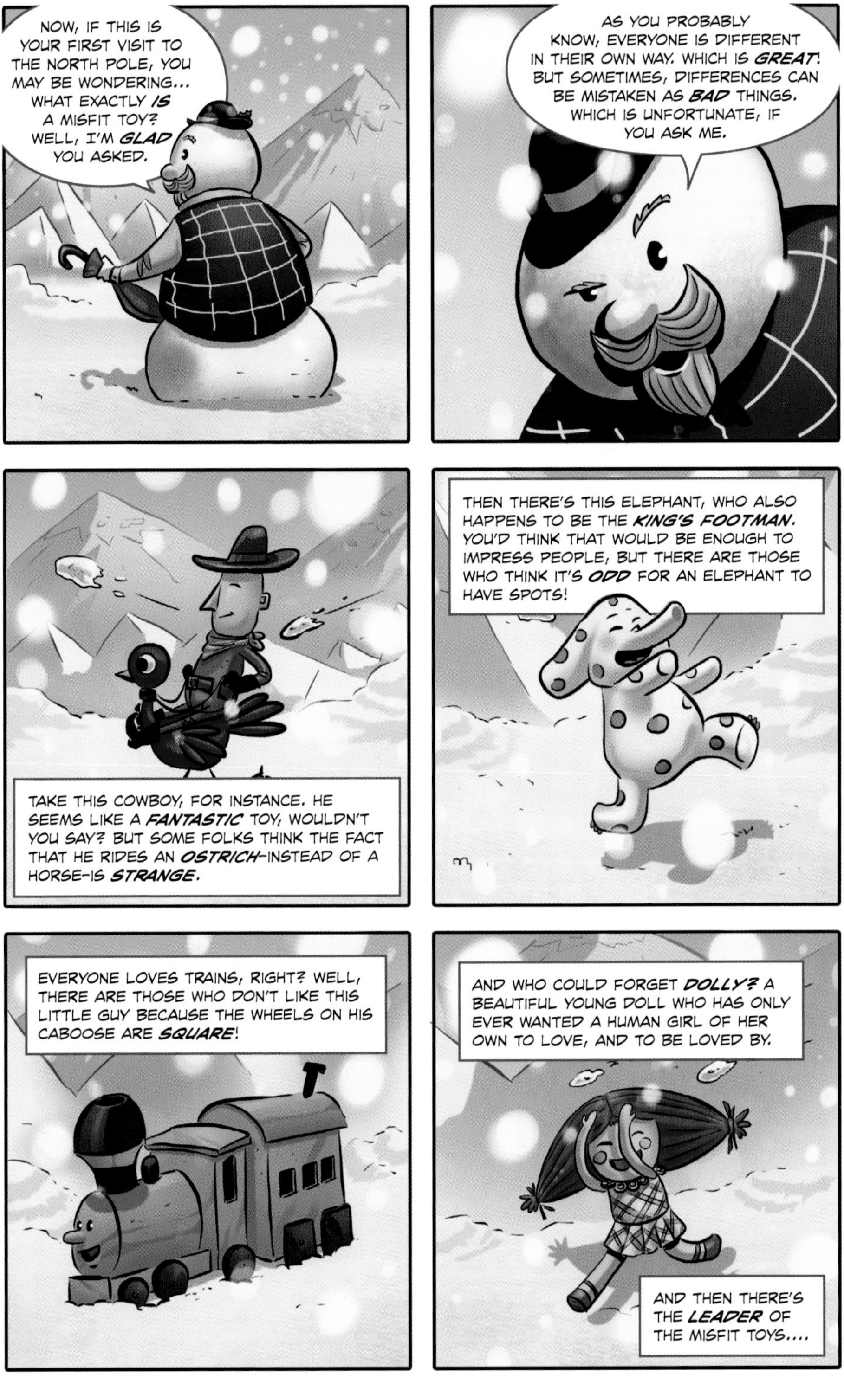
NOW, IF THIS IS YOUR FIRST VISIT TO THE NORTH POLE, YOU MAY BE WONDERING... WHAT EXACTLY *IS* A MISFIT TOY? WELL, I'M *GLAD* YOU ASKED.
AS YOU PROBABLY KNOW, EVERYONE IS DIFFERENT IN THEIR OWN WAY. WHICH IS *GREAT*! BUT SOMETIMES, DIFFERENCES CAN BE MISTAKEN AS *BAD* THINGS. WHICH IS UNFORTUNATE, IF YOU ASK ME.
TAKE THIS COWBOY, FOR INSTANCE. HE SEEMS LIKE A *FANTASTIC* TOY, WOULDN'T YOU SAY? BUT SOME FOLKS THINK THE FACT THAT HE RIDES AN *OSTRICH*–INSTEAD OF A HORSE–IS *STRANGE*.
THEN THERE'S THIS ELEPHANT, WHO ALSO HAPPENS TO BE THE *KING'S FOOTMAN*. YOU'D THINK THAT WOULD BE ENOUGH TO IMPRESS PEOPLE, BUT THERE ARE THOSE WHO THINK IT'S *ODD* FOR AN ELEPHANT TO HAVE SPOTS!
EVERYONE LOVES TRAINS, RIGHT? WELL, THERE ARE THOSE WHO DON'T LIKE THIS LITTLE GUY BECAUSE THE WHEELS ON HIS CABOOSE ARE *SQUARE*!
AND WHO COULD FORGET *DOLLY*? A BEAUTIFUL YOUNG DOLL WHO HAS ONLY EVER WANTED A HUMAN GIRL OF HER OWN TO LOVE, AND TO BE LOVED BY.
AND THEN THERE'S THE *LEADER* OF THE MISFIT TOYS....

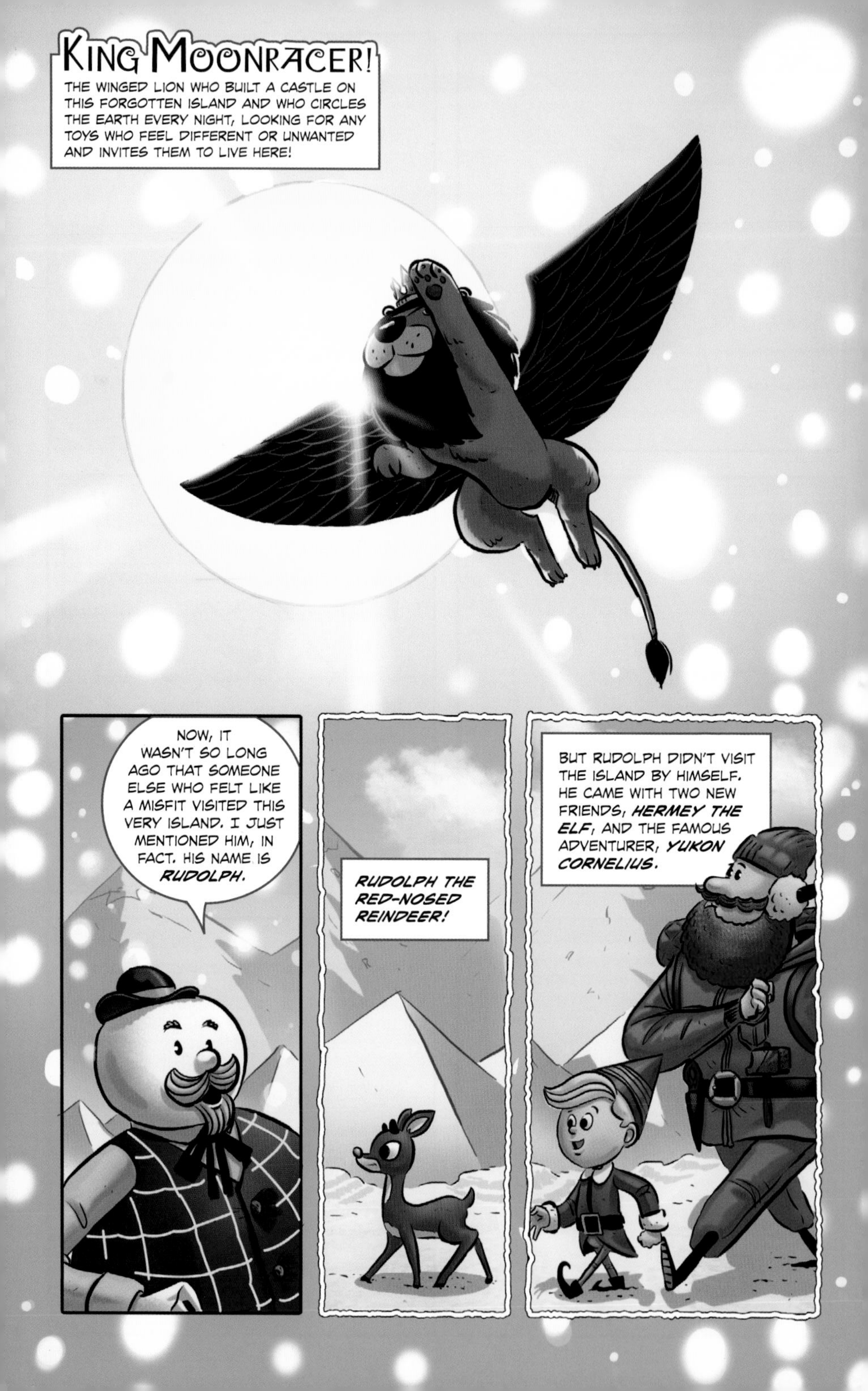
KING MOONRACER!
THE WINGED LION WHO BUILT A CASTLE ON THIS FORGOTTEN ISLAND AND WHO CIRCLES THE EARTH EVERY NIGHT, LOOKING FOR ANY TOYS WHO FEEL DIFFERENT OR UNWANTED AND INVITES THEM TO LIVE HERE!
NOW, IT WASN'T SO LONG AGO THAT SOMEONE ELSE WHO FELT LIKE A MISFIT VISITED THIS VERY ISLAND. I JUST MENTIONED HIM, IN FACT. HIS NAME IS *RUDOLPH*.
RUDOLPH THE RED-NOSED REINDEER!
BUT RUDOLPH DIDN'T VISIT THE ISLAND BY HIMSELF. HE CAME WITH TWO NEW FRIENDS, *HERMEY THE ELF*, AND THE FAMOUS ADVENTURER, *YUKON CORNELIUS*.

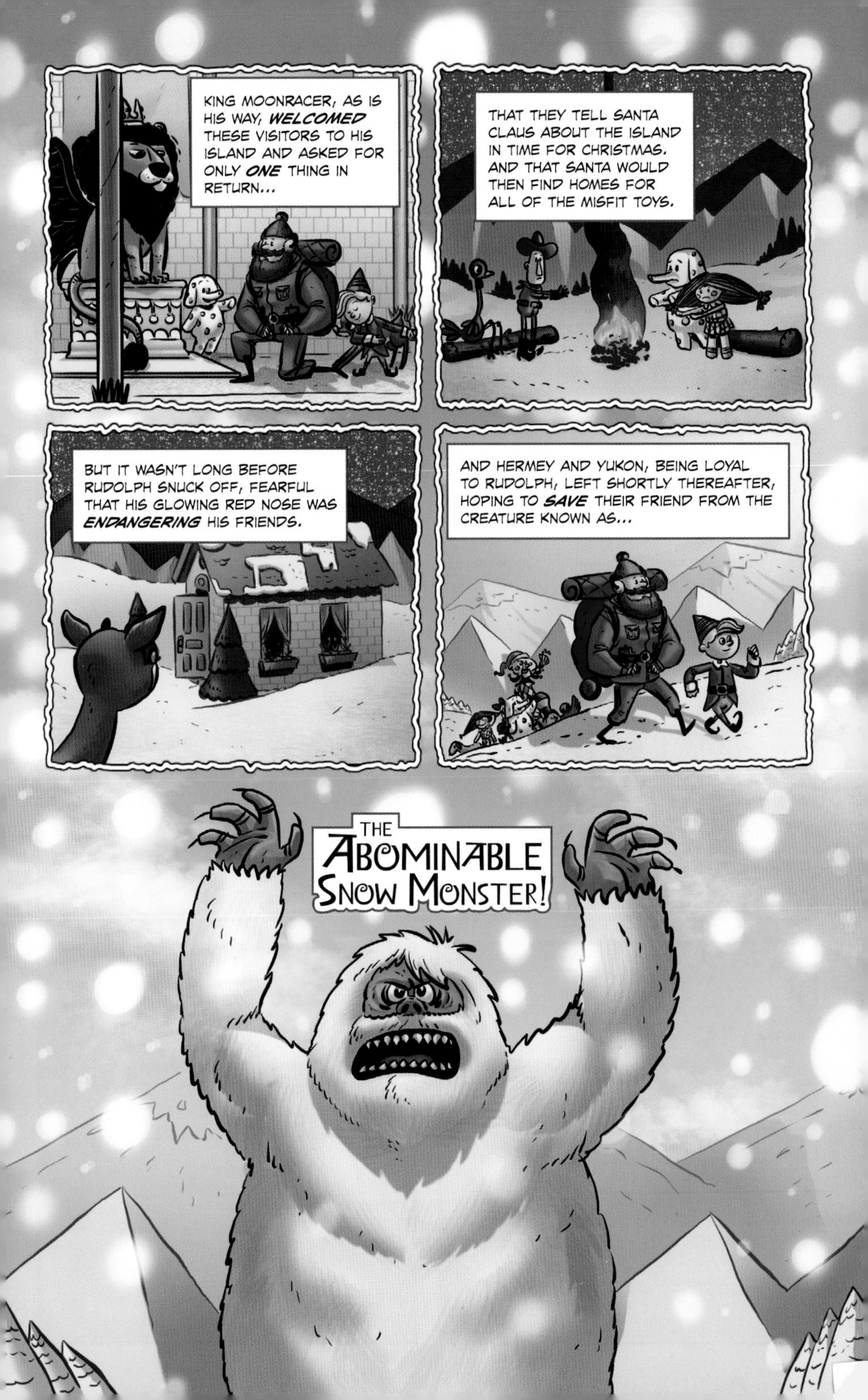
KING MOONRACER, AS IS HIS WAY, WELCOMED THESE VISITORS TO HIS ISLAND AND ASKED FOR ONLY ONE THING IN RETURN...
THAT THEY TELL SANTA CLAUS ABOUT THE ISLAND IN TIME FOR CHRISTMAS. AND THAT SANTA WOULD THEN FIND HOMES FOR ALL OF THE MISFIT TOYS.
BUT IT WASN'T LONG BEFORE RUDOLPH SNUCK OFF, FEARFUL THAT HIS GLOWING RED NOSE WAS ENDANGERING HIS FRIENDS.
AND HERMEY AND YUKON, BEING LOYAL TO RUDOLPH, LEFT SHORTLY THEREAFTER, HOPING TO SAVE THEIR FRIEND FROM THE CREATURE KNOWN AS...
THE ABOMINABLE SNOW MONSTER!

NOW, EVER SINCE RUDOLPH, HERMEY, AND YUKON LEFT THE ISLAND, THERE'S BEEN A SENSE OF *HOPE* AMONG THE TOYS. A FEELING THAT SANTA MIGHT COME AFTER ALL....

BUT THERE WAS *ONE* TOY WHO WAS EVEN MORE HOPEFUL THAN THE REST...

AND HIS NAME IS *CHARLIE-IN-THE-BOX.*

SANTA IS GOING TO COME FOR US! I'M JUST SURE OF IT! AND WHEN HE DOES, I'LL HAVE MY VERY OWN HOME TO—

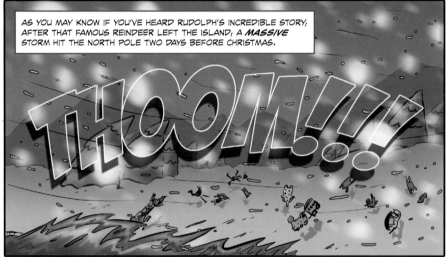

AS YOU MAY KNOW IF YOU'VE HEARD RUDOLPH'S INCREDIBLE STORY, AFTER THAT FAMOUS REINDEER LEFT THE ISLAND, A *MASSIVE* STORM HIT THE NORTH POLE TWO DAYS BEFORE CHRISTMAS.

THOOM!!!

AND *NO* PLACE WAS HARDER HIT THAN THE ISLAND OF MISFIT TOYS.

KRIKK!

UH-OH.

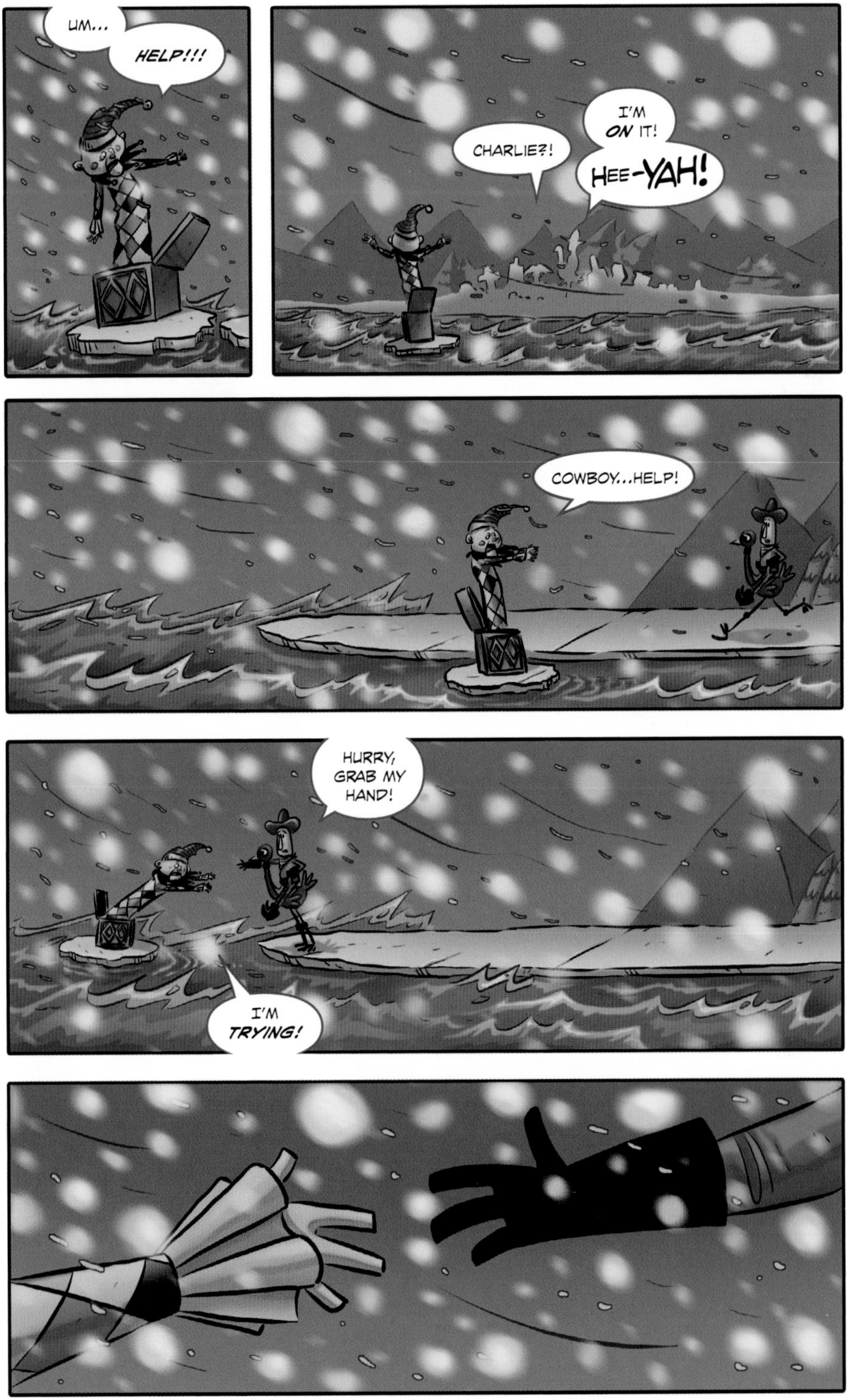
UM...
HELP!!!
CHARLIE?!
I'M ON IT!
HEE-YAH!
COWBOY...HELP!
HURRY, GRAB MY HAND!
I'M TRYING!

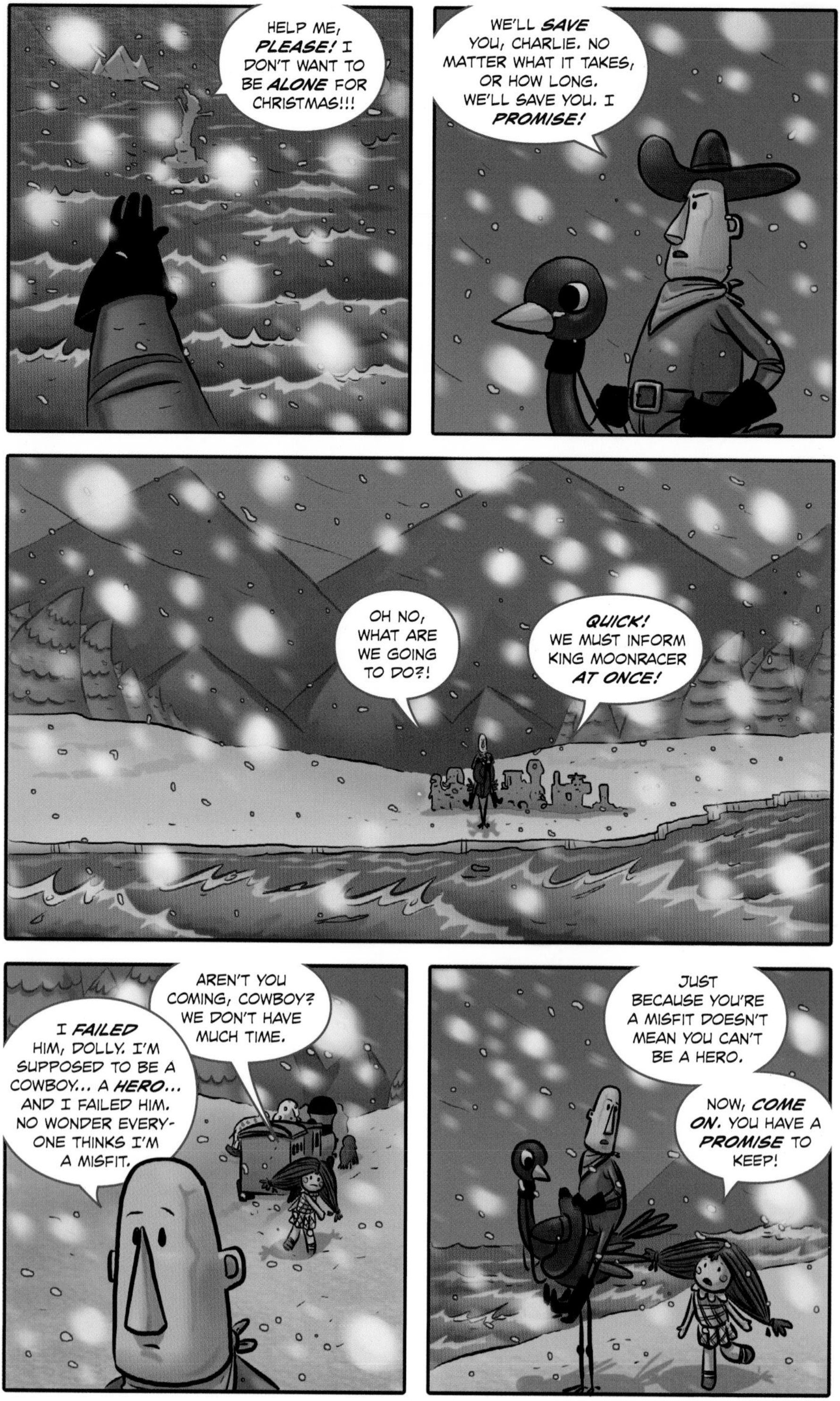
HELP ME, PLEASE! I DON'T WANT TO BE ALONE FOR CHRISTMAS!!!
WE'LL SAVE YOU, CHARLIE. NO MATTER WHAT IT TAKES, OR HOW LONG. WE'LL SAVE YOU. I PROMISE!
OH NO, WHAT ARE WE GOING TO DO?!
QUICK! WE MUST INFORM KING MOONRACER AT ONCE!
AREN'T YOU COMING, COWBOY? WE DON'T HAVE MUCH TIME.
I FAILED HIM, DOLLY. I'M SUPPOSED TO BE A COWBOY... A HERO... AND I FAILED HIM. NO WONDER EVERY-ONE THINKS I'M A MISFIT.
JUST BECAUSE YOU'RE A MISFIT DOESN'T MEAN YOU CAN'T BE A HERO.
NOW, COME ON. YOU HAVE A PROMISE TO KEEP!

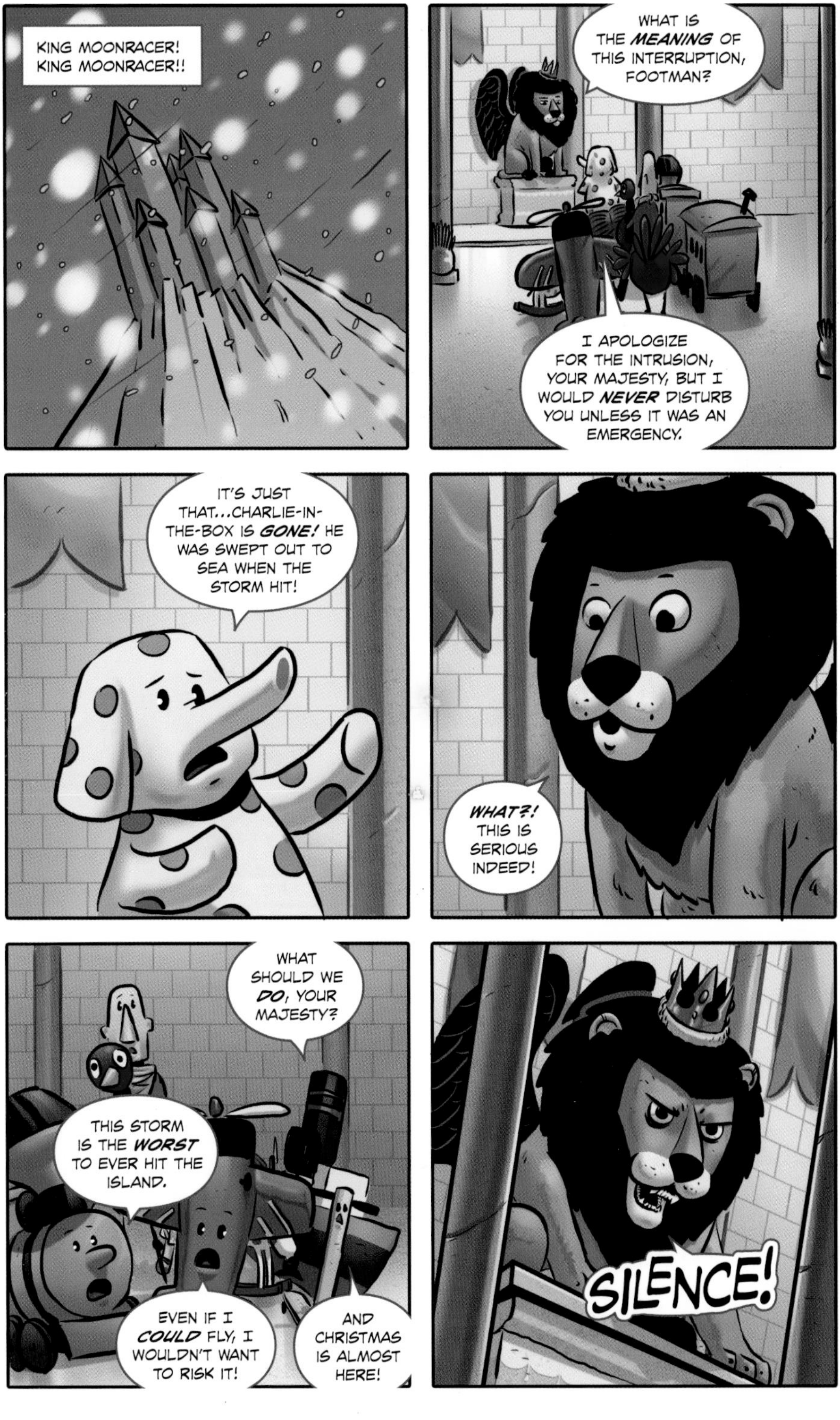
KING MOONRACER!
KING MOONRACER!!
WHAT IS THE MEANING OF THIS INTERRUPTION, FOOTMAN?
I APOLOGIZE FOR THE INTRUSION, YOUR MAJESTY, BUT I WOULD NEVER DISTURB YOU UNLESS IT WAS AN EMERGENCY.
IT'S JUST THAT...CHARLIE-IN-THE-BOX IS GONE! HE WAS SWEPT OUT TO SEA WHEN THE STORM HIT!
WHAT?! THIS IS SERIOUS INDEED!
WHAT SHOULD WE DO, YOUR MAJESTY?
THIS STORM IS THE WORST TO EVER HIT THE ISLAND.
EVEN IF I COULD FLY, I WOULDN'T WANT TO RISK IT!
AND CHRISTMAS IS ALMOST HERE!
SILENCE!

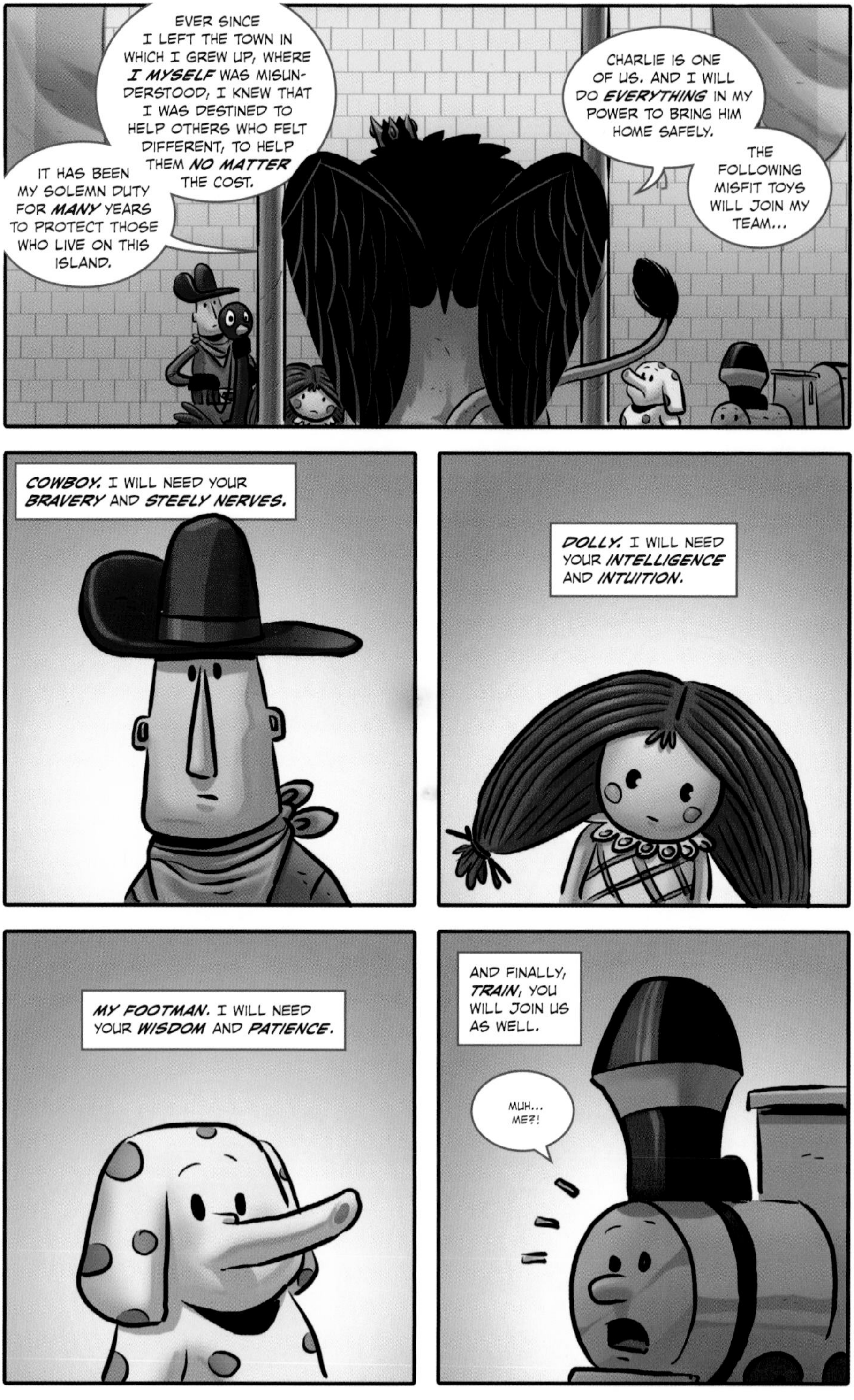
EVER SINCE I LEFT THE TOWN IN WHICH I GREW UP, WHERE I MYSELF WAS MISUNDERSTOOD, I KNEW THAT I WAS DESTINED TO HELP OTHERS WHO FELT DIFFERENT, TO HELP THEM NO MATTER THE COST.
IT HAS BEEN MY SOLEMN DUTY FOR MANY YEARS TO PROTECT THOSE WHO LIVE ON THIS ISLAND.
CHARLIE IS ONE OF US. AND I WILL DO EVERYTHING IN MY POWER TO BRING HIM HOME SAFELY.
THE FOLLOWING MISFIT TOYS WILL JOIN MY TEAM...
COWBOY. I WILL NEED YOUR BRAVERY AND STEELY NERVES.
DOLLY. I WILL NEED YOUR INTELLIGENCE AND INTUITION.
MY FOOTMAN. I WILL NEED YOUR WISDOM AND PATIENCE.
AND FINALLY, TRAIN, YOU WILL JOIN US AS WELL.
MUH... ME?!

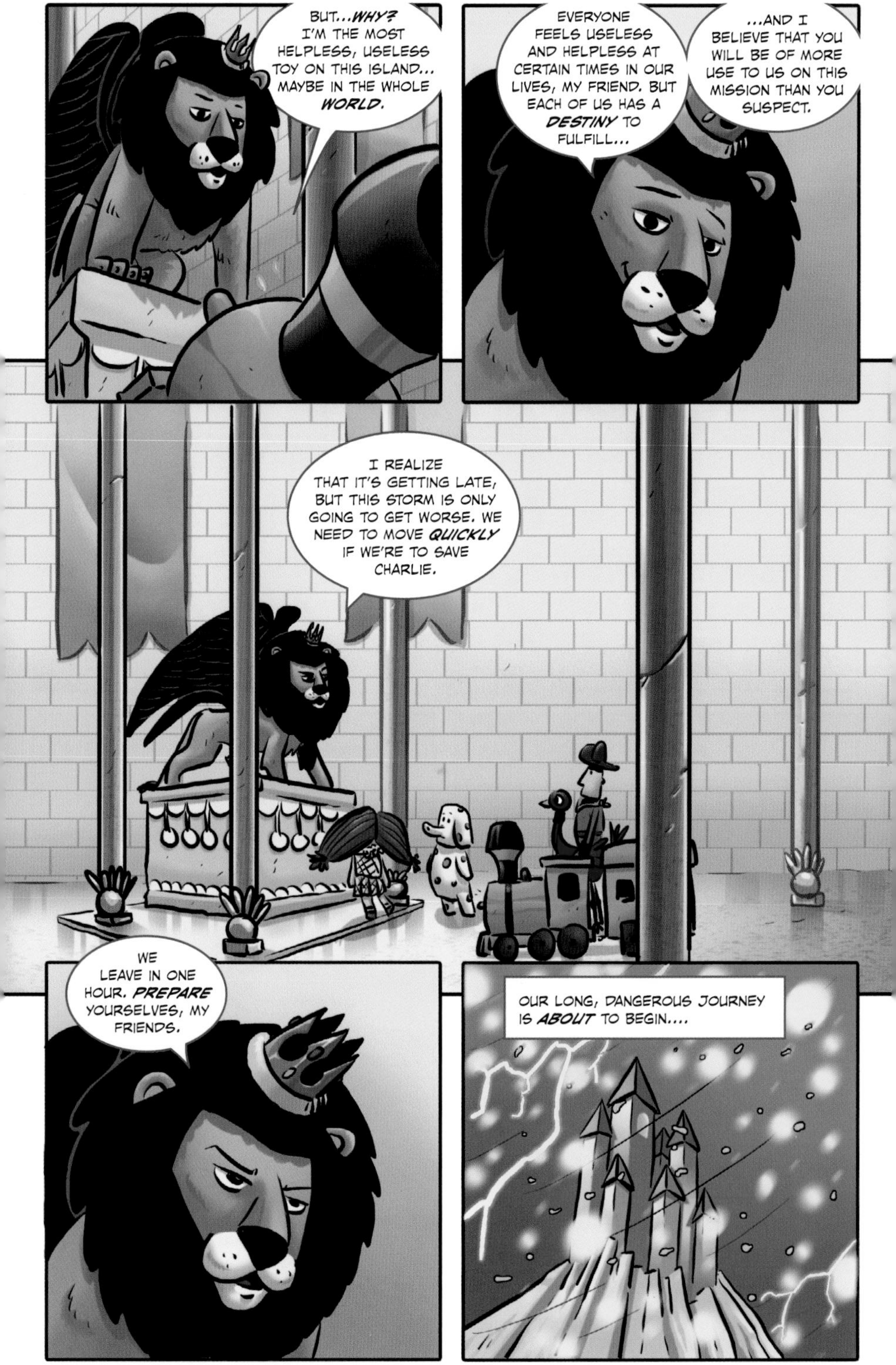
BUT...*WHY?* I'M THE MOST HELPLESS, USELESS TOY ON THIS ISLAND... MAYBE IN THE WHOLE *WORLD*.
EVERYONE FEELS USELESS AND HELPLESS AT CERTAIN TIMES IN OUR LIVES, MY FRIEND. BUT EACH OF US HAS A *DESTINY* TO FULFILL...
...AND I BELIEVE THAT YOU WILL BE OF MORE USE TO US ON THIS MISSION THAN YOU SUSPECT.
I REALIZE THAT IT'S GETTING LATE, BUT THIS STORM IS ONLY GOING TO GET WORSE. WE NEED TO MOVE *QUICKLY* IF WE'RE TO SAVE CHARLIE.
WE LEAVE IN ONE HOUR. *PREPARE* YOURSELVES, MY FRIENDS.
OUR LONG, DANGEROUS JOURNEY IS *ABOUT* TO BEGIN....

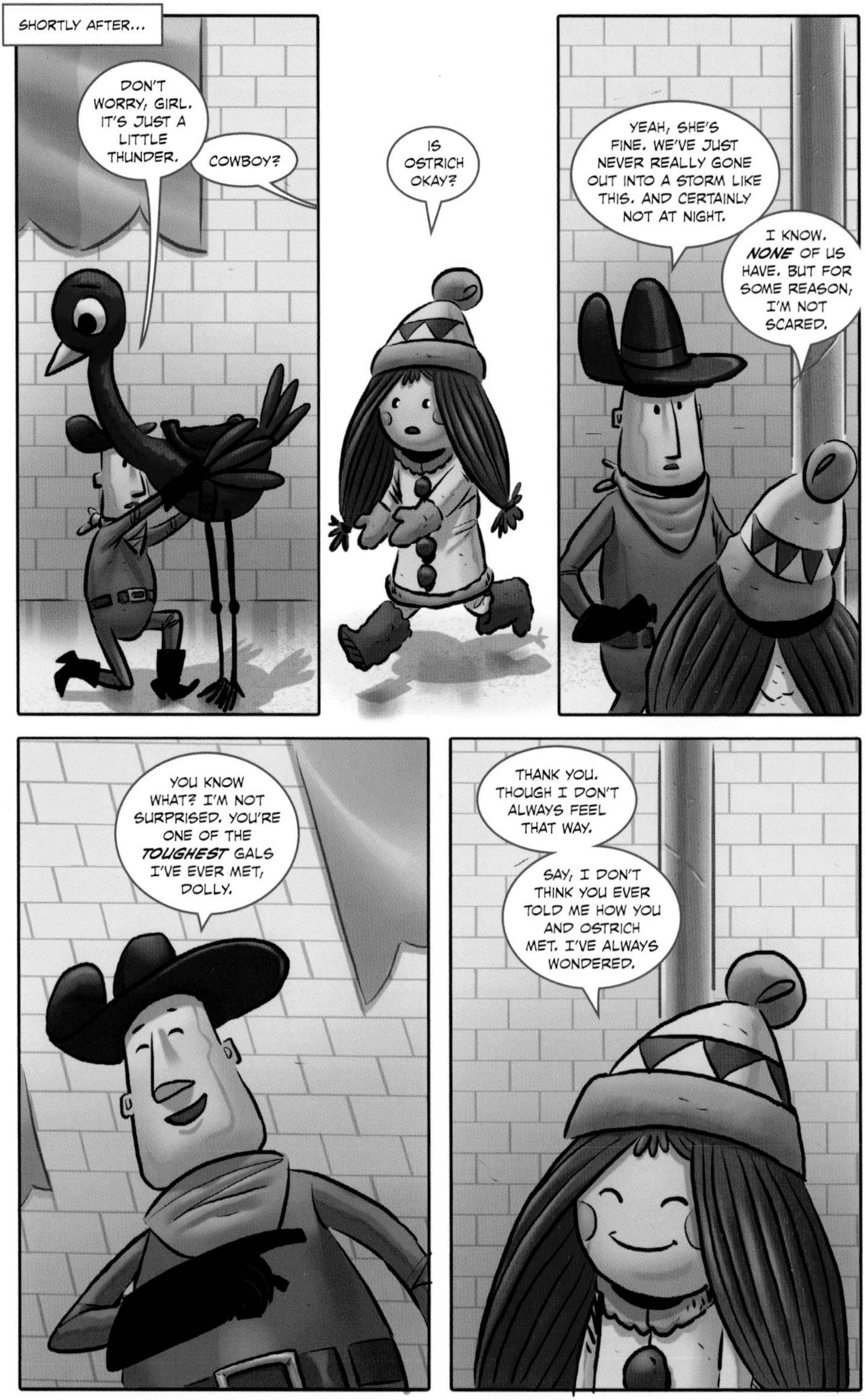
SHORTLY AFTER...
DON'T WORRY, GIRL. IT'S JUST A LITTLE THUNDER.
COWBOY?
IS OSTRICH OKAY?
YEAH, SHE'S FINE. WE'VE JUST NEVER REALLY GONE OUT INTO A STORM LIKE THIS. AND CERTAINLY NOT AT NIGHT.
I KNOW. NONE OF US HAVE. BUT FOR SOME REASON, I'M NOT SCARED.
YOU KNOW WHAT? I'M NOT SURPRISED. YOU'RE ONE OF THE TOUGHEST GALS I'VE EVER MET, DOLLY.
THANK YOU. THOUGH I DON'T ALWAYS FEEL THAT WAY.
SAY, I DON'T THINK YOU EVER TOLD ME HOW YOU AND OSTRICH MET. I'VE ALWAYS WONDERED.

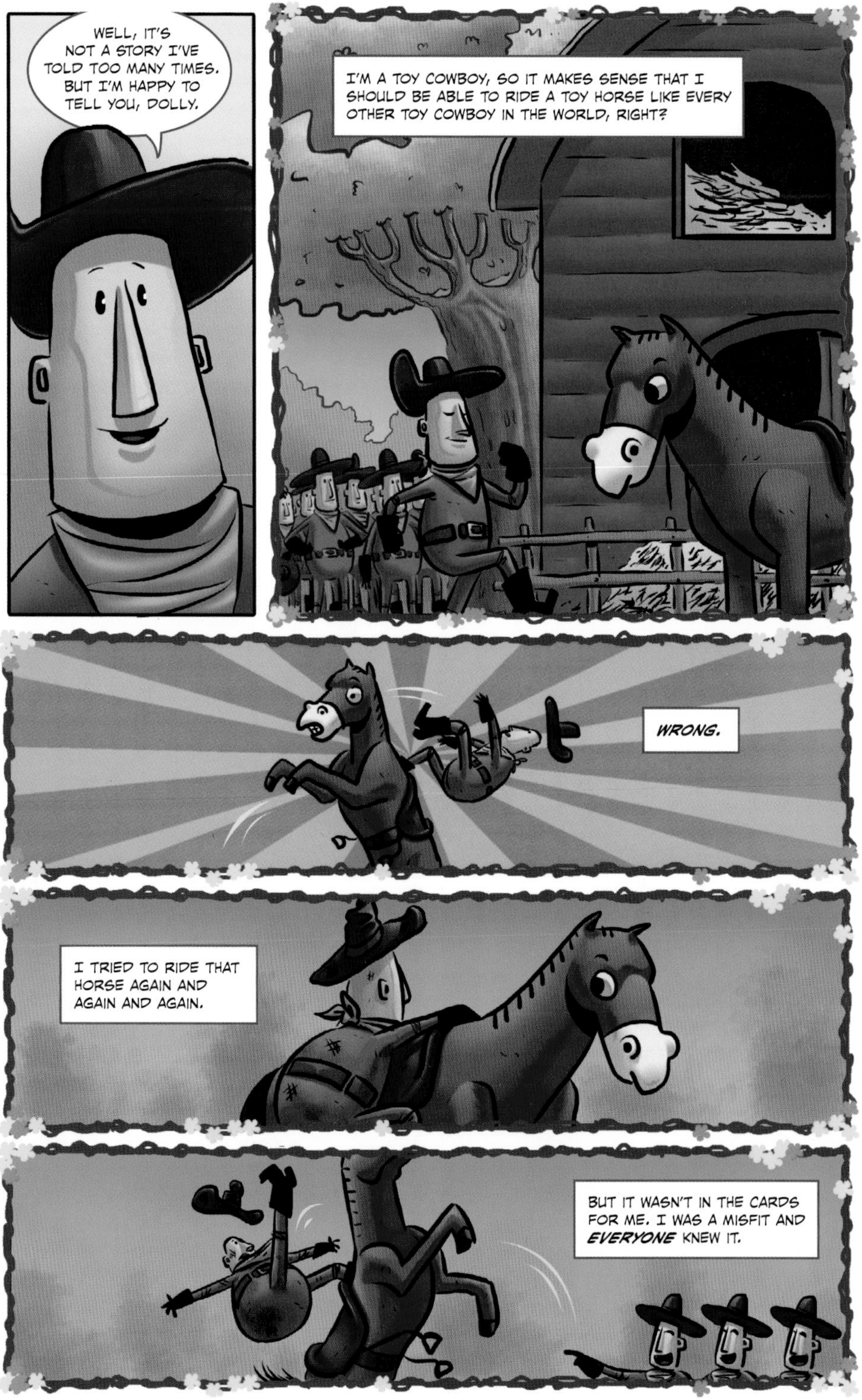
WELL, IT'S NOT A STORY I'VE TOLD TOO MANY TIMES. BUT I'M HAPPY TO TELL YOU, DOLLY.
I'M A TOY COWBOY, SO IT MAKES SENSE THAT I SHOULD BE ABLE TO RIDE A TOY HORSE LIKE EVERY OTHER TOY COWBOY IN THE WORLD, RIGHT?
WRONG.
I TRIED TO RIDE THAT HORSE AGAIN AND AGAIN AND AGAIN.
BUT IT WASN'T IN THE CARDS FOR ME. I WAS A MISFIT AND *EVERYONE* KNEW IT.

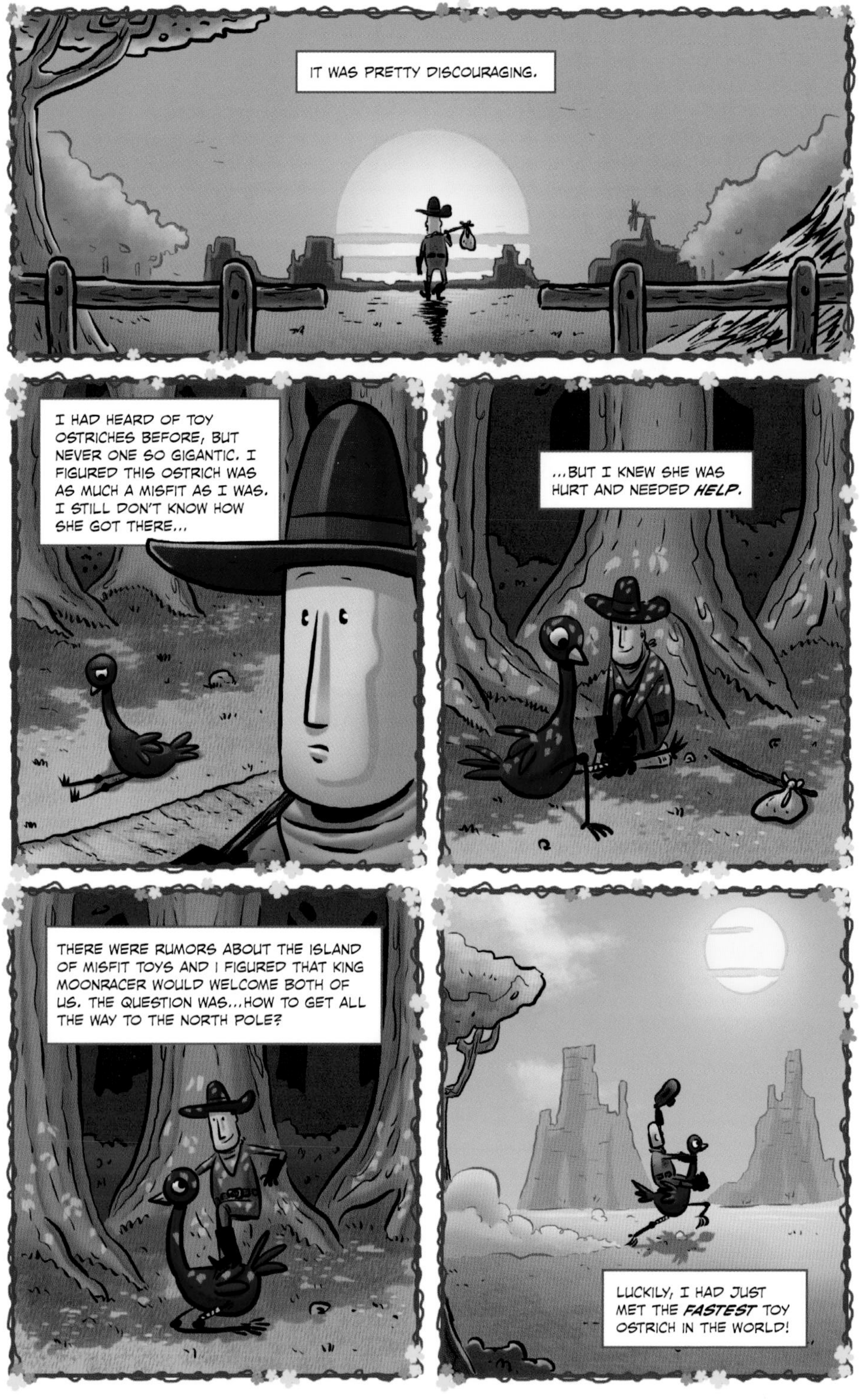
IT WAS PRETTY DISCOURAGING.
I HAD HEARD OF TOY OSTRICHES BEFORE, BUT NEVER ONE SO GIGANTIC. I FIGURED THIS OSTRICH WAS AS MUCH A MISFIT AS I WAS. I STILL DON'T KNOW HOW SHE GOT THERE...
...BUT I KNEW SHE WAS HURT AND NEEDED *HELP.*
THERE WERE RUMORS ABOUT THE ISLAND OF MISFIT TOYS AND I FIGURED THAT KING MOONRACER WOULD WELCOME BOTH OF US. THE QUESTION WAS...HOW TO GET ALL THE WAY TO THE NORTH POLE?
LUCKILY, I HAD JUST MET THE *FASTEST* TOY OSTRICH IN THE WORLD!

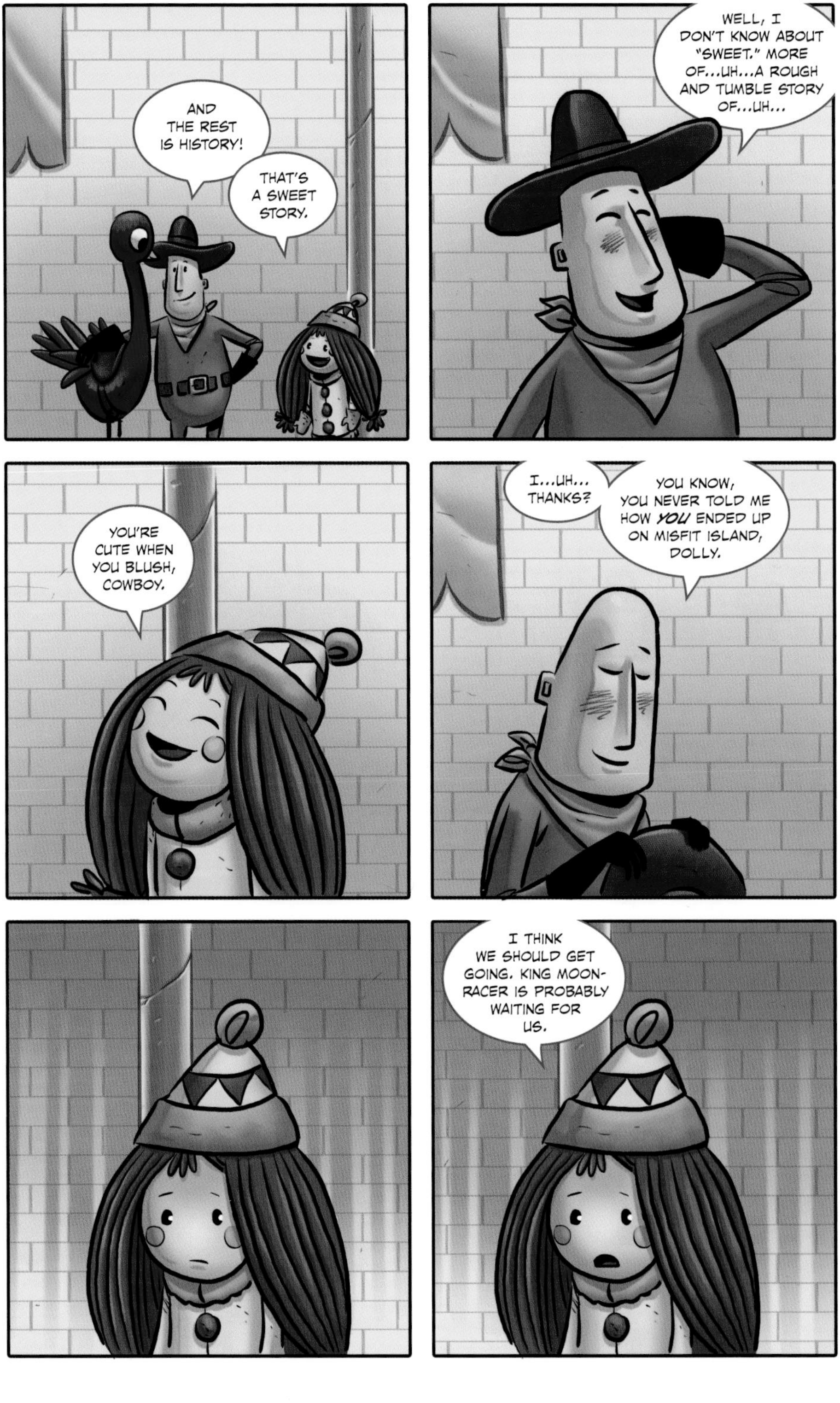
AND THE REST IS HISTORY!
THAT'S A SWEET STORY.
WELL, I DON'T KNOW ABOUT "SWEET." MORE OF...UH...A ROUGH AND TUMBLE STORY OF...UH...
YOU'RE CUTE WHEN YOU BLUSH, COWBOY.
I...UH... THANKS?
YOU KNOW, YOU NEVER TOLD ME HOW *YOU* ENDED UP ON MISFIT ISLAND, DOLLY.
I THINK WE SHOULD GET GOING. KING MOON-RACER IS PROBABLY WAITING FOR US.

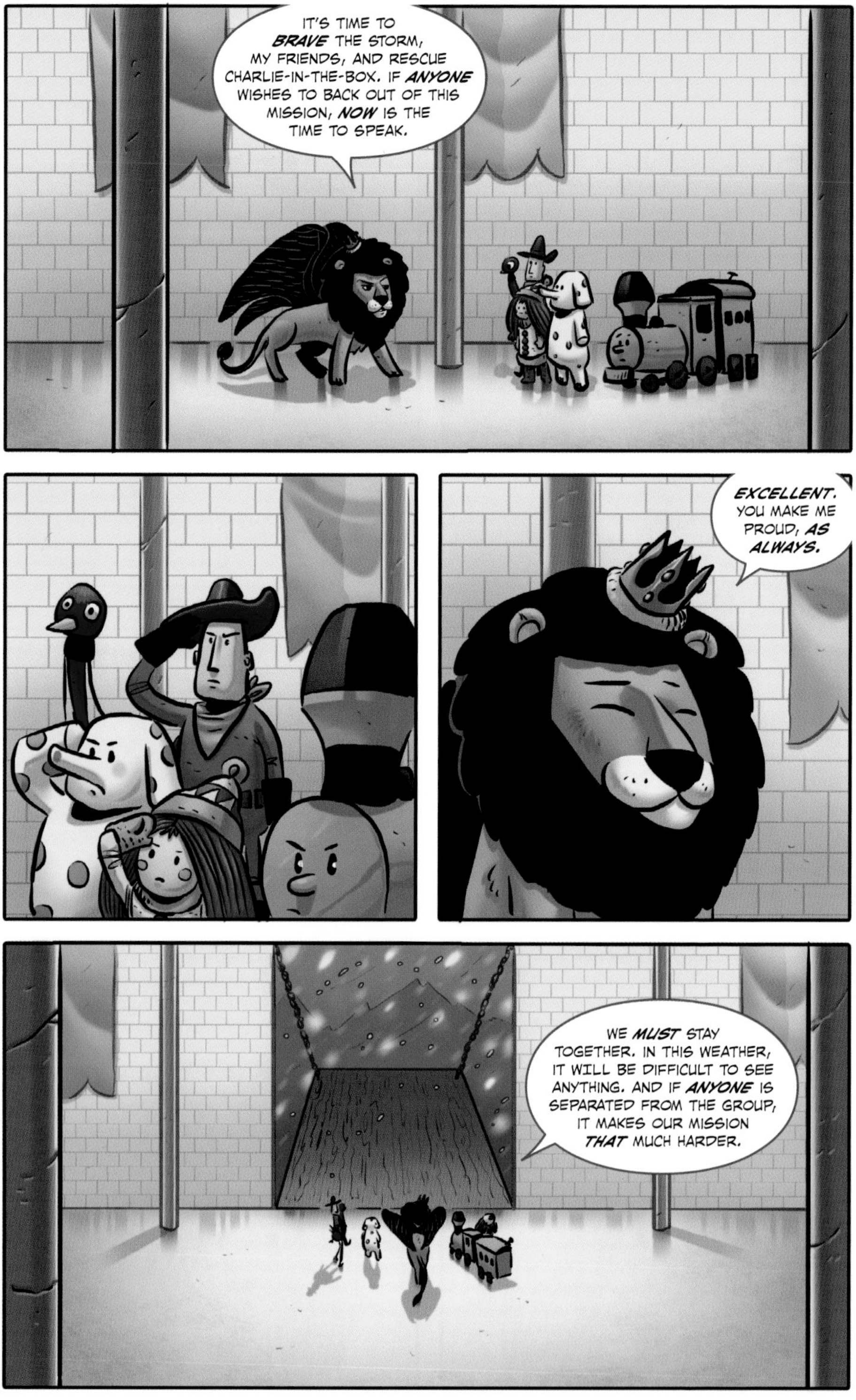

IT'S TIME TO BRAVE THE STORM, MY FRIENDS, AND RESCUE CHARLIE-IN-THE-BOX. IF ANYONE WISHES TO BACK OUT OF THIS MISSION, NOW IS THE TIME TO SPEAK.
EXCELLENT. YOU MAKE ME PROUD, AS ALWAYS.
WE MUST STAY TOGETHER. IN THIS WEATHER, IT WILL BE DIFFICULT TO SEE ANYTHING. AND IF ANYONE IS SEPARATED FROM THE GROUP, IT MAKES OUR MISSION THAT MUCH HARDER.

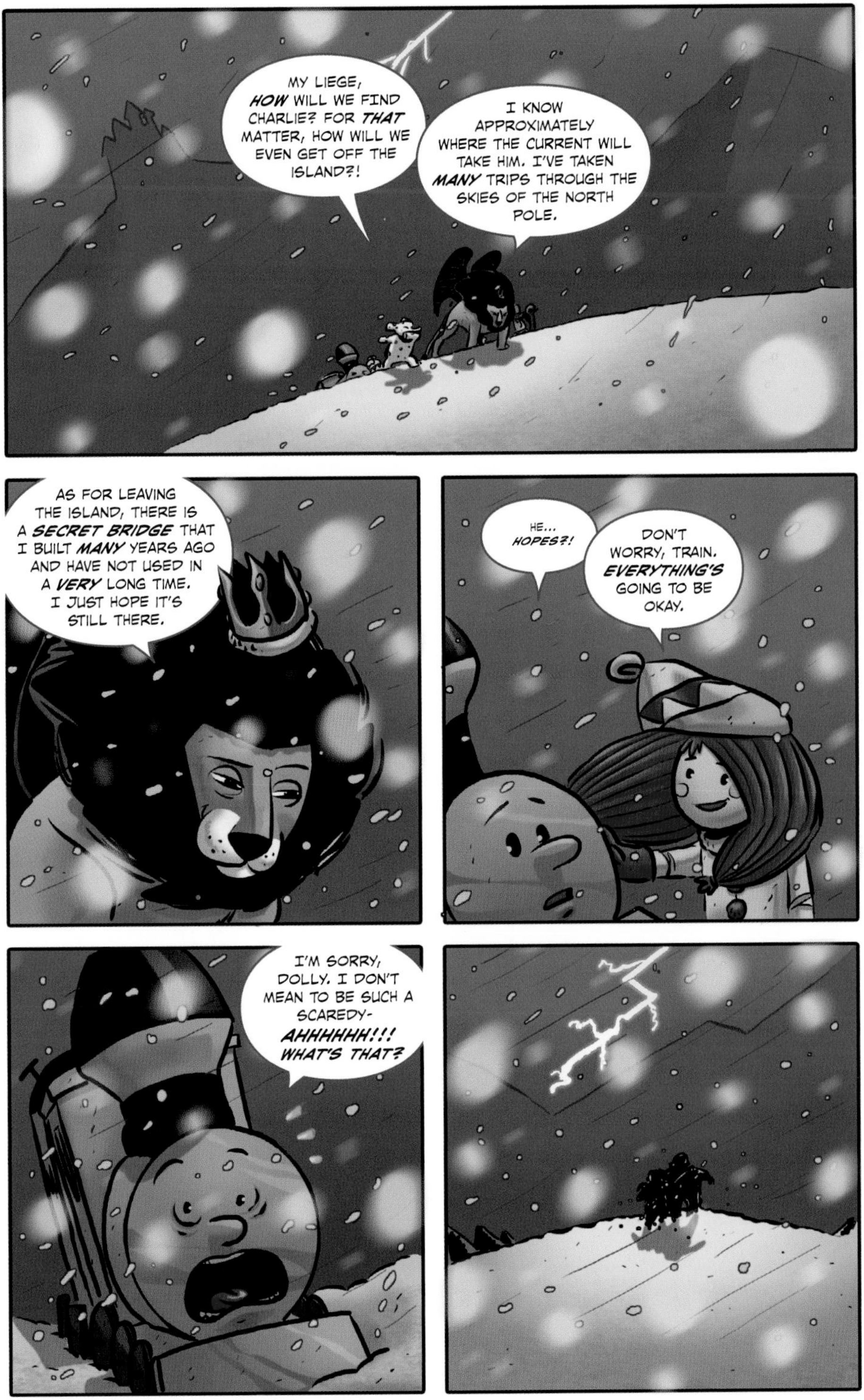
MY LIEGE, HOW WILL WE FIND CHARLIE? FOR THAT MATTER, HOW WILL WE EVEN GET OFF THE ISLAND?!
I KNOW APPROXIMATELY WHERE THE CURRENT WILL TAKE HIM. I'VE TAKEN MANY TRIPS THROUGH THE SKIES OF THE NORTH POLE.
AS FOR LEAVING THE ISLAND, THERE IS A SECRET BRIDGE THAT I BUILT MANY YEARS AGO AND HAVE NOT USED IN A VERY LONG TIME. I JUST HOPE IT'S STILL THERE.
HE... HOPES?!
DON'T WORRY, TRAIN. EVERYTHING'S GOING TO BE OKAY.
I'M SORRY, DOLLY. I DON'T MEAN TO BE SUCH A SCAREDY- AHHHHHH!!! WHAT'S THAT?

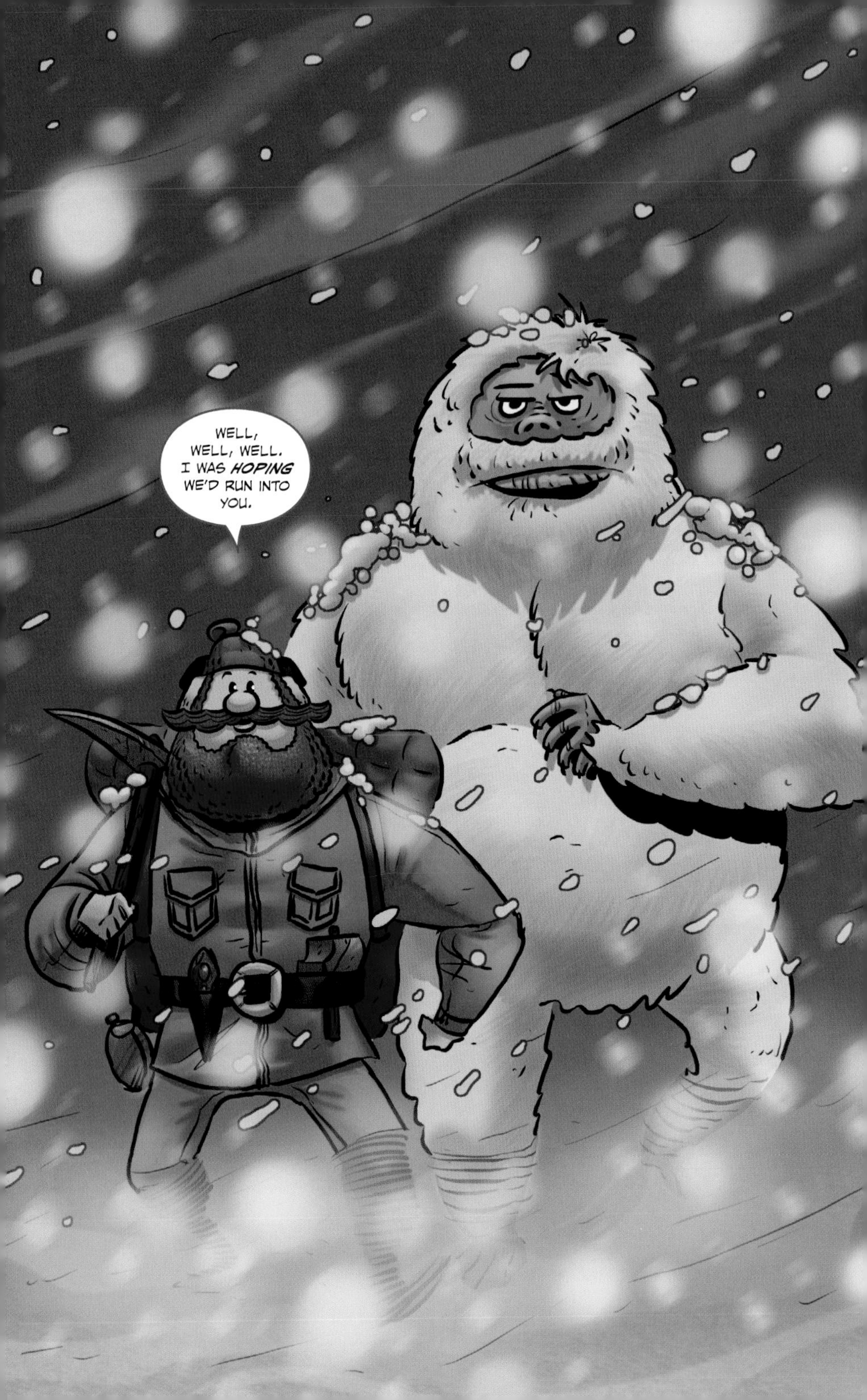
WELL, WELL, WELL. I WAS HOPING WE'D RUN INTO YOU.

CHAPTER TWO

SEPARATED!

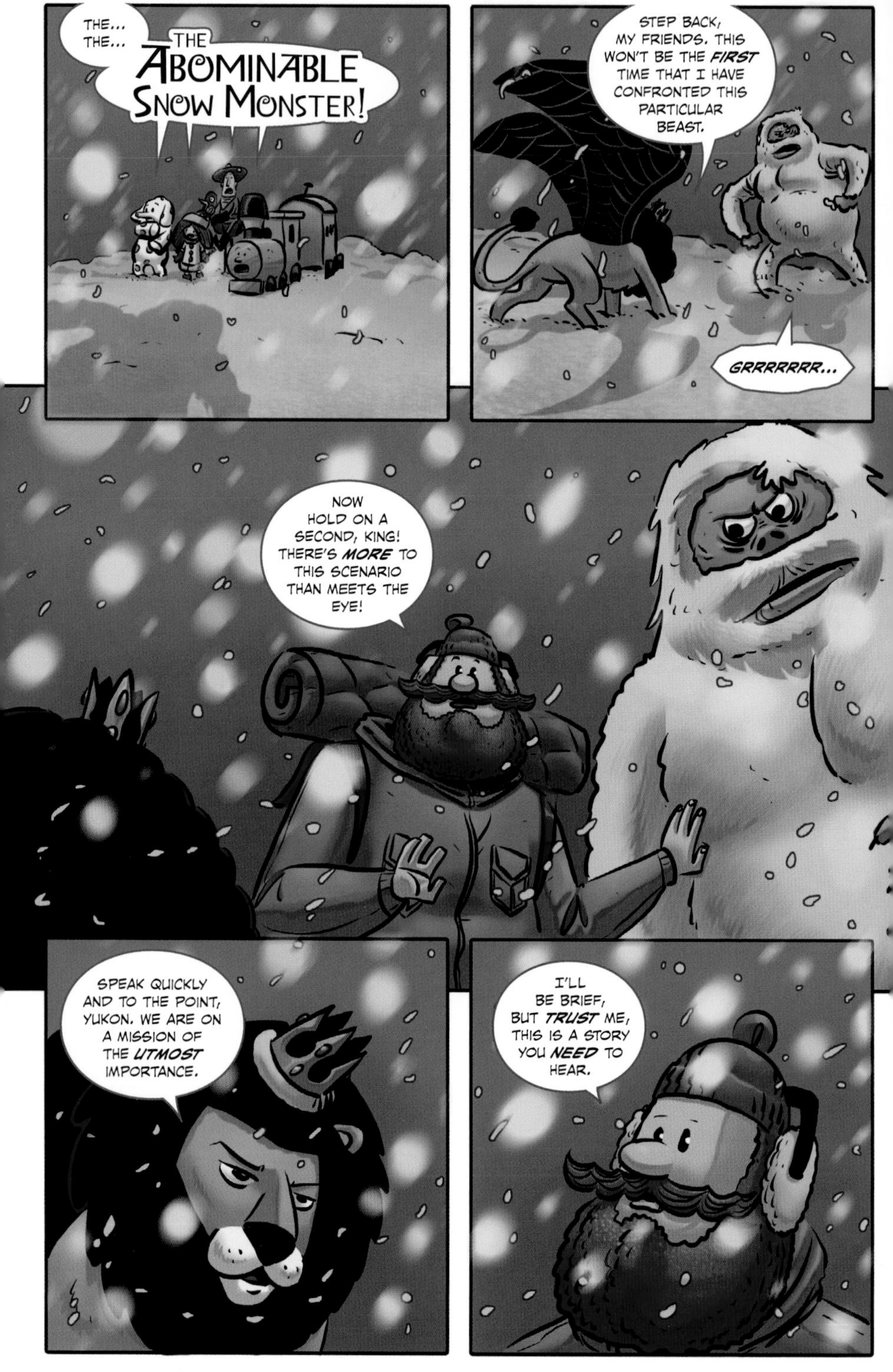
THE... THE... THE ABOMINABLE SNOW MONSTER!
STEP BACK, MY FRIENDS. THIS WON'T BE THE FIRST TIME THAT I HAVE CONFRONTED THIS PARTICULAR BEAST.
GRRRRRRR...
NOW HOLD ON A SECOND, KING! THERE'S MORE TO THIS SCENARIO THAN MEETS THE EYE!
SPEAK QUICKLY AND TO THE POINT, YUKON. WE ARE ON A MISSION OF THE UTMOST IMPORTANCE.
I'LL BE BRIEF, BUT TRUST ME, THIS IS A STORY YOU NEED TO HEAR.

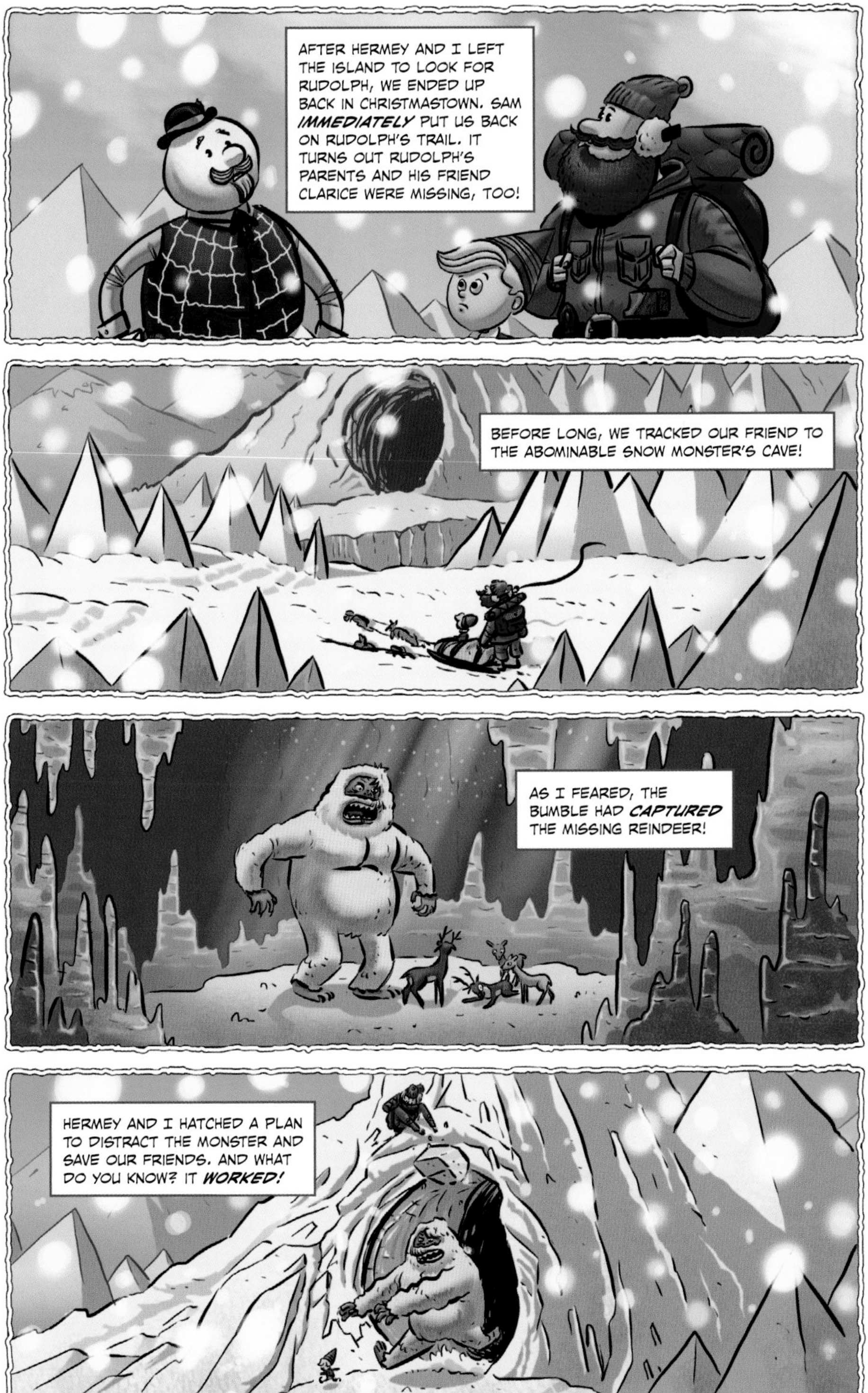
AFTER HERMEY AND I LEFT THE ISLAND TO LOOK FOR RUDOLPH, WE ENDED UP BACK IN CHRISTMASTOWN. SAM IMMEDIATELY PUT US BACK ON RUDOLPH'S TRAIL. IT TURNS OUT RUDOLPH'S PARENTS AND HIS FRIEND CLARICE WERE MISSING, TOO!
BEFORE LONG, WE TRACKED OUR FRIEND TO THE ABOMINABLE SNOW MONSTER'S CAVE!
AS I FEARED, THE BUMBLE HAD CAPTURED THE MISSING REINDEER!
HERMEY AND I HATCHED A PLAN TO DISTRACT THE MONSTER AND SAVE OUR FRIENDS. AND WHAT DO YOU KNOW? IT WORKED!

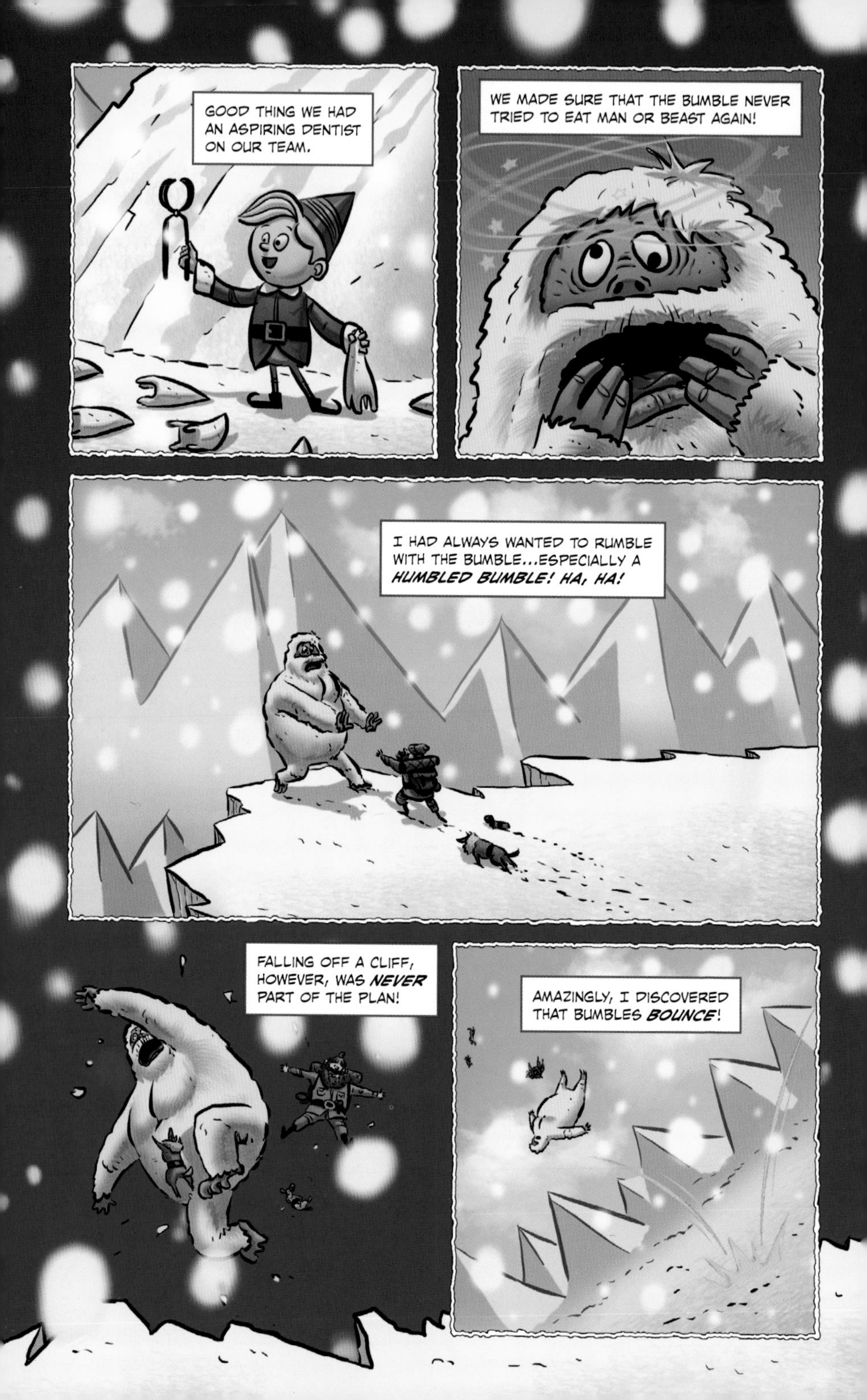
GOOD THING WE HAD AN ASPIRING DENTIST ON OUR TEAM.
WE MADE SURE THAT THE BUMBLE NEVER TRIED TO EAT MAN OR BEAST AGAIN!
I HAD ALWAYS WANTED TO RUMBLE WITH THE BUMBLE...ESPECIALLY A HUMBLED BUMBLE! HA, HA!
FALLING OFF A CLIFF, HOWEVER, WAS NEVER PART OF THE PLAN!
AMAZINGLY, I DISCOVERED THAT BUMBLES BOUNCE!

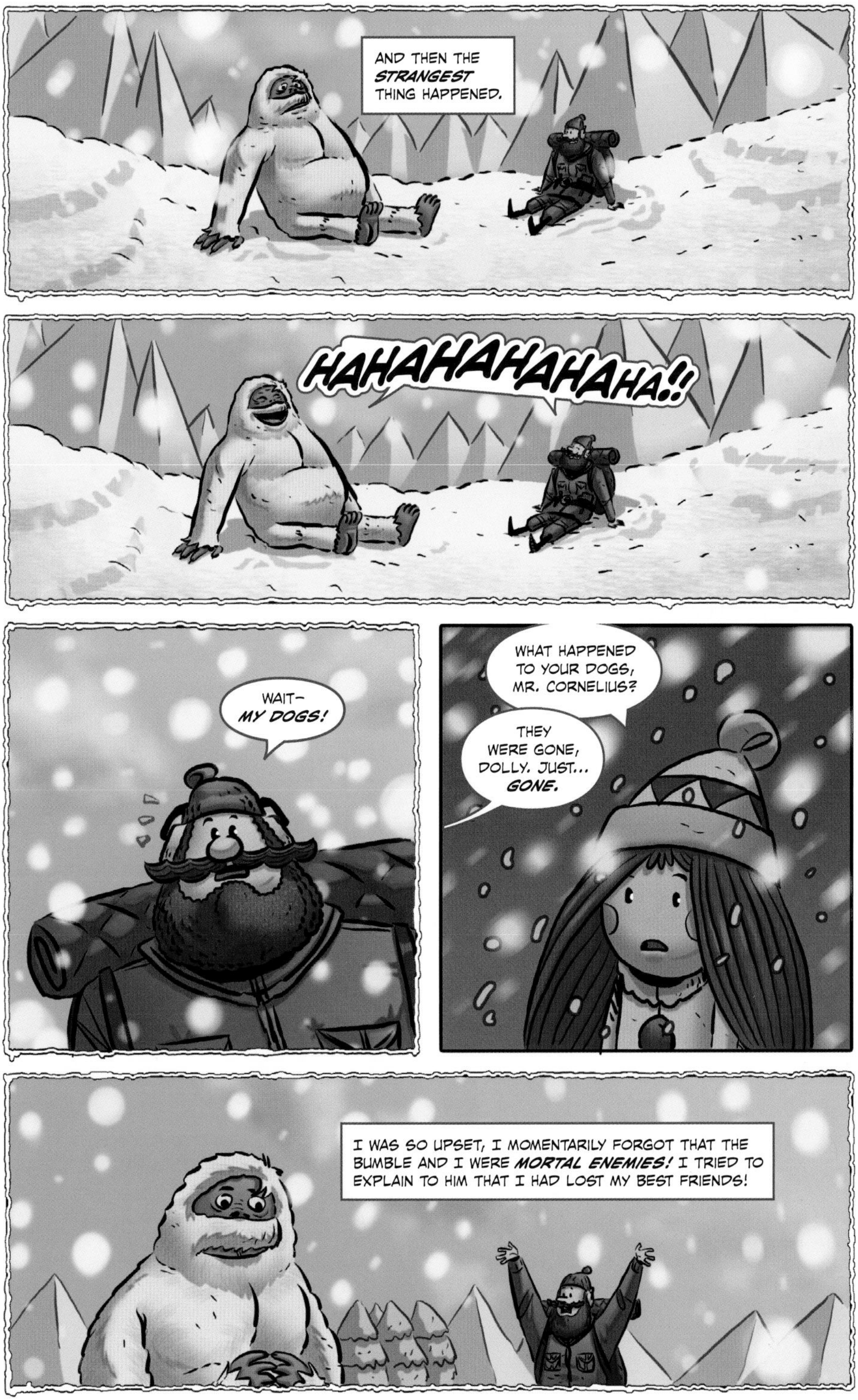
AND THEN THE *STRANGEST* THING HAPPENED.
HAHAHAHAHAHAHA!!
WAIT— *MY DOGS!*
WHAT HAPPENED TO YOUR DOGS, MR. CORNELIUS?
THEY WERE GONE, DOLLY. JUST... *GONE.*
I WAS SO UPSET, I MOMENTARILY FORGOT THAT THE BUMBLE AND I WERE *MORTAL ENEMIES!* I TRIED TO EXPLAIN TO HIM THAT I HAD LOST MY BEST FRIENDS!

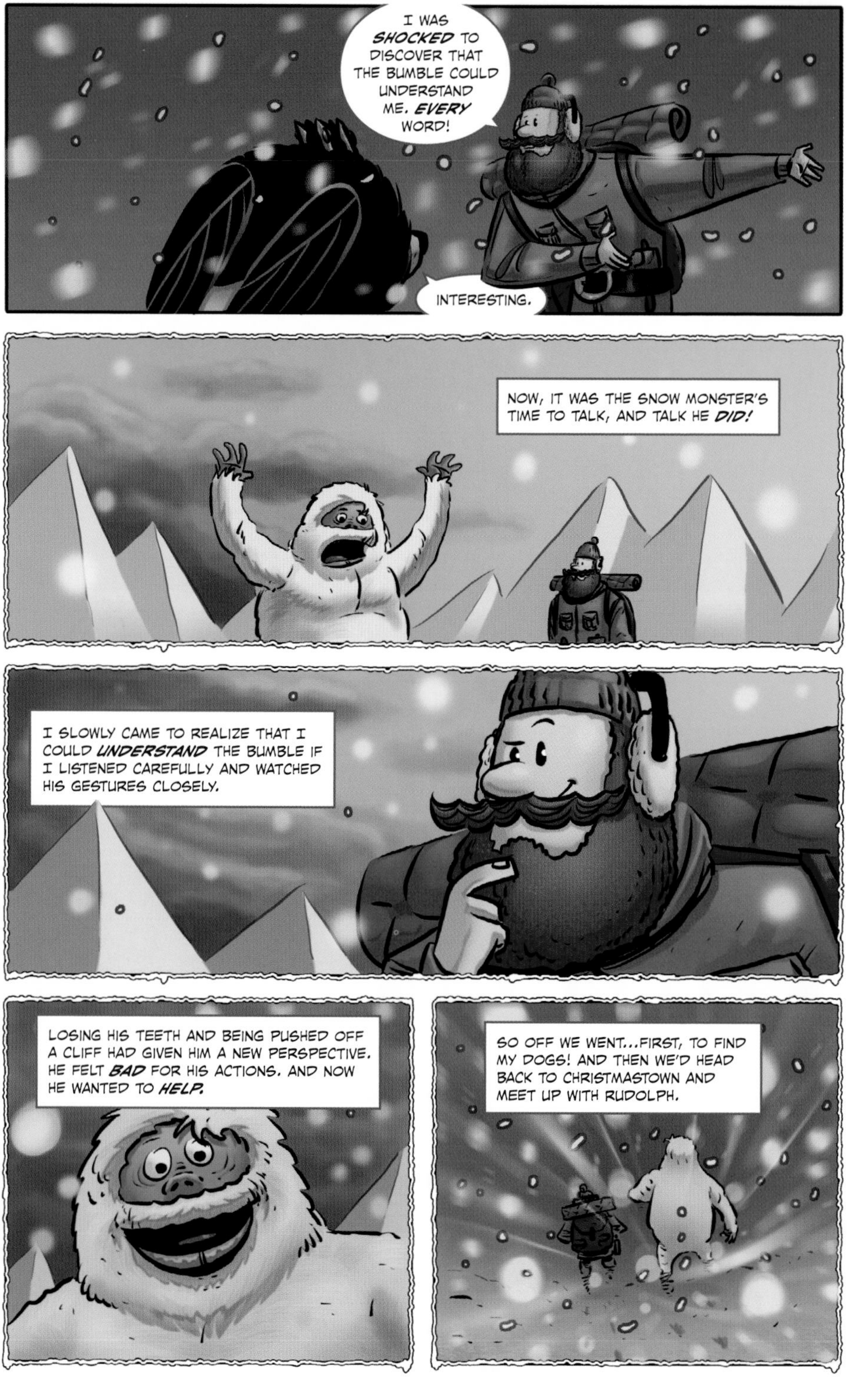
I WAS SHOCKED TO DISCOVER THAT THE BUMBLE COULD UNDERSTAND ME. EVERY WORD!
INTERESTING.
NOW, IT WAS THE SNOW MONSTER'S TIME TO TALK, AND TALK HE DID!
I SLOWLY CAME TO REALIZE THAT I COULD UNDERSTAND THE BUMBLE IF I LISTENED CAREFULLY AND WATCHED HIS GESTURES CLOSELY.
LOSING HIS TEETH AND BEING PUSHED OFF A CLIFF HAD GIVEN HIM A NEW PERSPECTIVE. HE FELT BAD FOR HIS ACTIONS. AND NOW HE WANTED TO HELP.
SO OFF WE WENT...FIRST, TO FIND MY DOGS! AND THEN WE'D HEAD BACK TO CHRISTMASTOWN AND MEET UP WITH RUDOLPH.

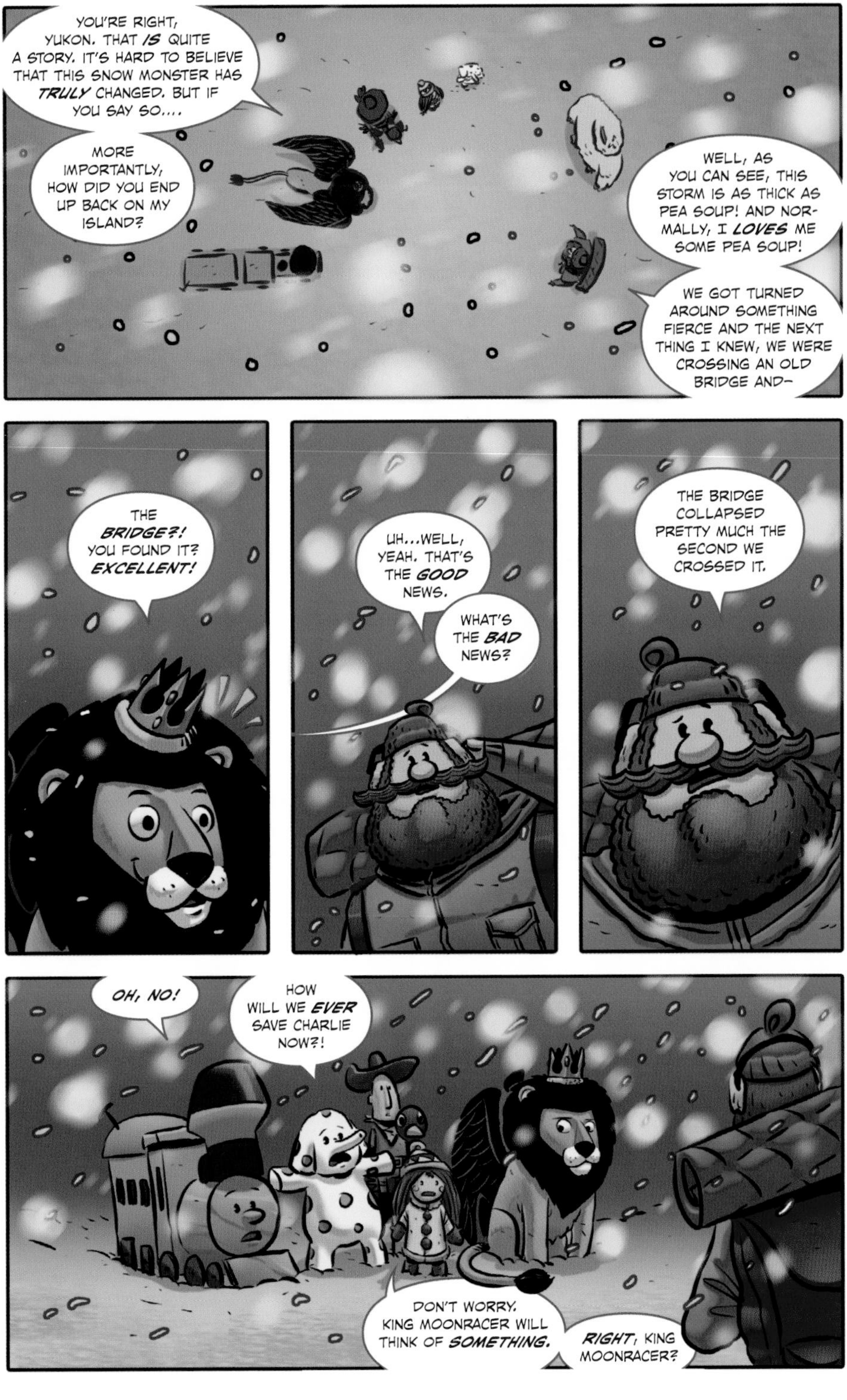
YOU'RE RIGHT, YUKON. THAT *IS* QUITE A STORY. IT'S HARD TO BELIEVE THAT THIS SNOW MONSTER HAS *TRULY* CHANGED. BUT IF YOU SAY SO....
MORE IMPORTANTLY, HOW DID YOU END UP BACK ON MY ISLAND?
WELL, AS YOU CAN SEE, THIS STORM IS AS THICK AS PEA SOUP! AND NOR-MALLY, I *LOVES* ME SOME PEA SOUP!
WE GOT TURNED AROUND SOMETHING FIERCE AND THE NEXT THING I KNEW, WE WERE CROSSING AN OLD BRIDGE AND—
THE *BRIDGE?!* YOU FOUND IT? *EXCELLENT!*
UH...WELL, YEAH. THAT'S THE *GOOD* NEWS.
WHAT'S THE *BAD* NEWS?
THE BRIDGE COLLAPSED PRETTY MUCH THE SECOND WE CROSSED IT.
OH, NO!
HOW WILL WE *EVER* SAVE CHARLIE NOW?!
DON'T WORRY. KING MOONRACER WILL THINK OF *SOMETHING.*
RIGHT, KING MOONRACER?

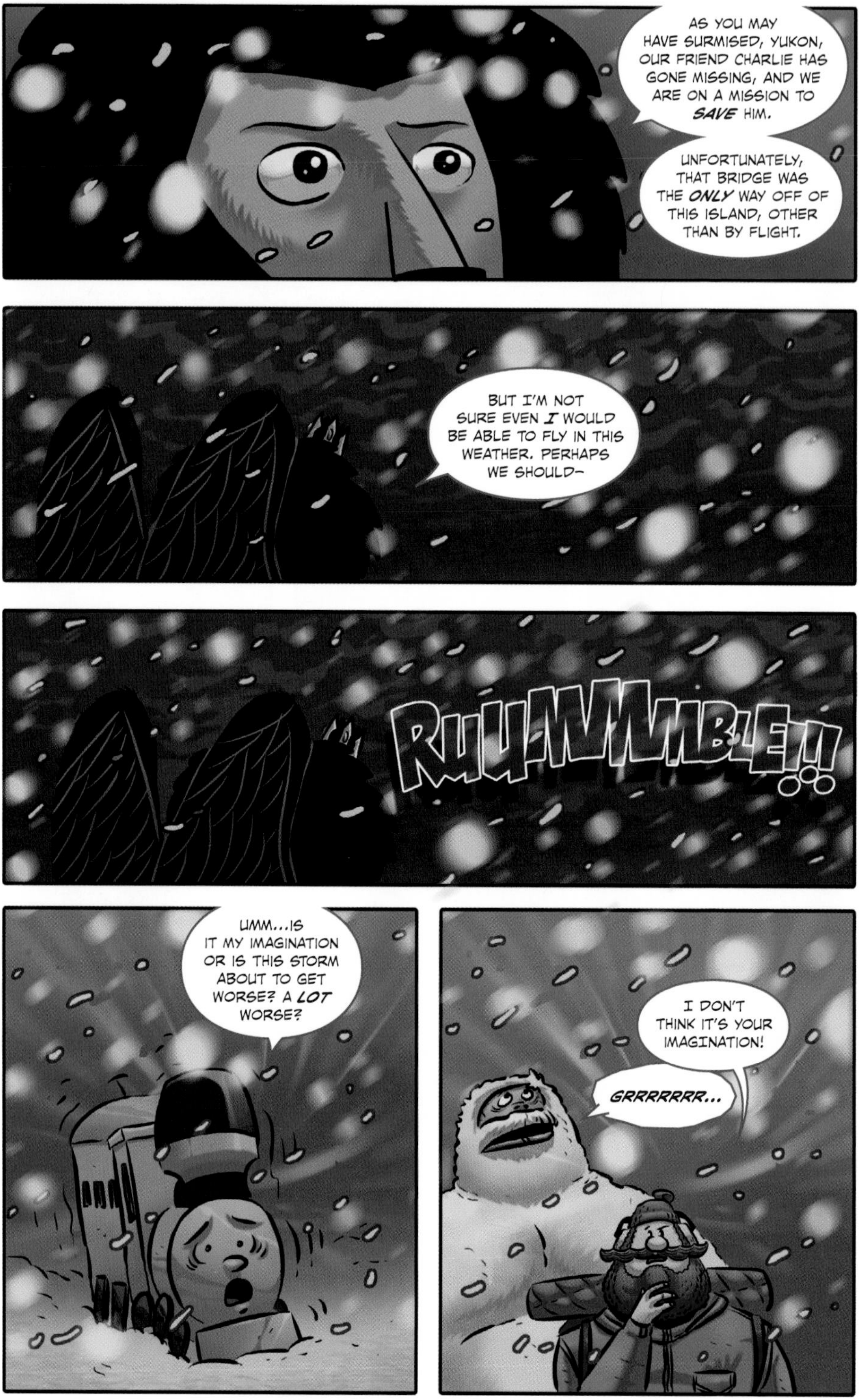
AS YOU MAY HAVE SURMISED, YUKON, OUR FRIEND CHARLIE HAS GONE MISSING, AND WE ARE ON A MISSION TO SAVE HIM.
UNFORTUNATELY, THAT BRIDGE WAS THE ONLY WAY OFF OF THIS ISLAND, OTHER THAN BY FLIGHT.
BUT I'M NOT SURE EVEN I WOULD BE ABLE TO FLY IN THIS WEATHER. PERHAPS WE SHOULD–
RUUMMMBLE!!!
UMM...IS IT MY IMAGINATION OR IS THIS STORM ABOUT TO GET WORSE? A LOT WORSE?
I DON'T THINK IT'S YOUR IMAGINATION!
GRRRRRRR...

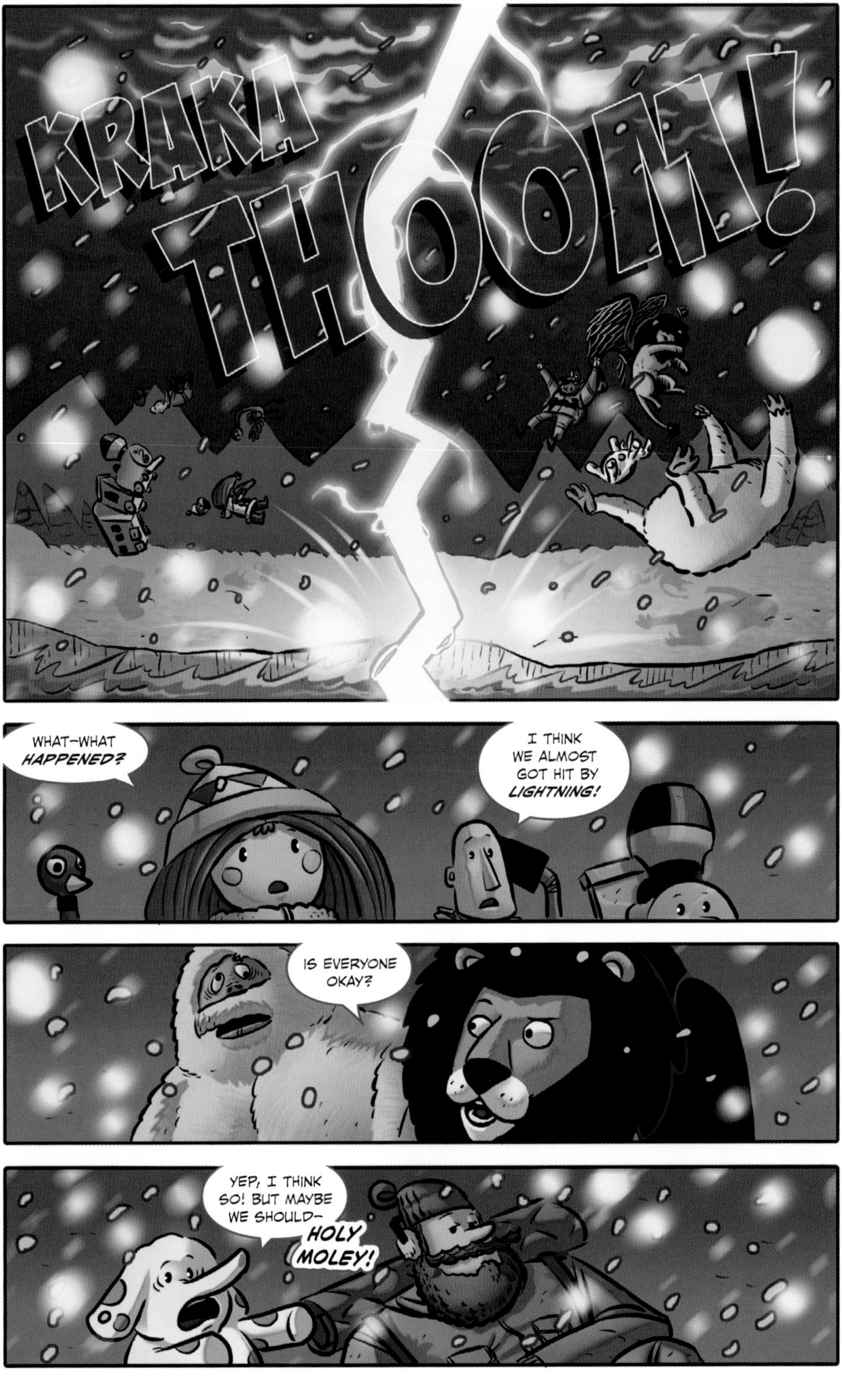
KRAKA
THOOM!
WHAT—WHAT HAPPENED?
I THINK WE ALMOST GOT HIT BY LIGHTNING!
IS EVERYONE OKAY?
YEP, I THINK SO! BUT MAYBE WE SHOULD—
HOLY MOLEY!

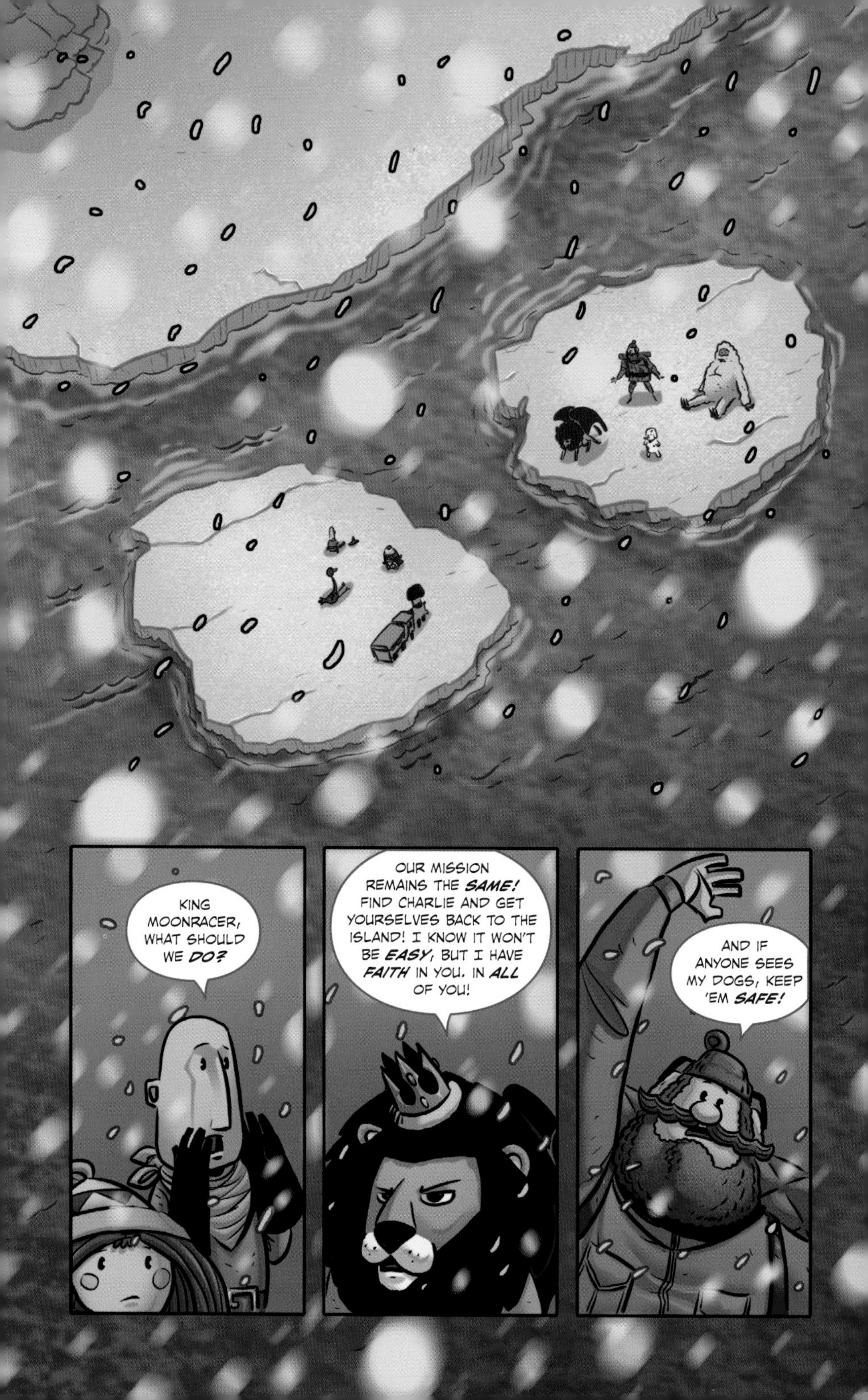
KING MOONRACER, WHAT SHOULD WE DO?
OUR MISSION REMAINS THE SAME! FIND CHARLIE AND GET YOURSELVES BACK TO THE ISLAND! I KNOW IT WON'T BE EASY, BUT I HAVE FAITH IN YOU. IN ALL OF YOU!
AND IF ANYONE SEES MY DOGS, KEEP 'EM SAFE!

CHAPTER THREE

DANGER AT EVERY TURN!

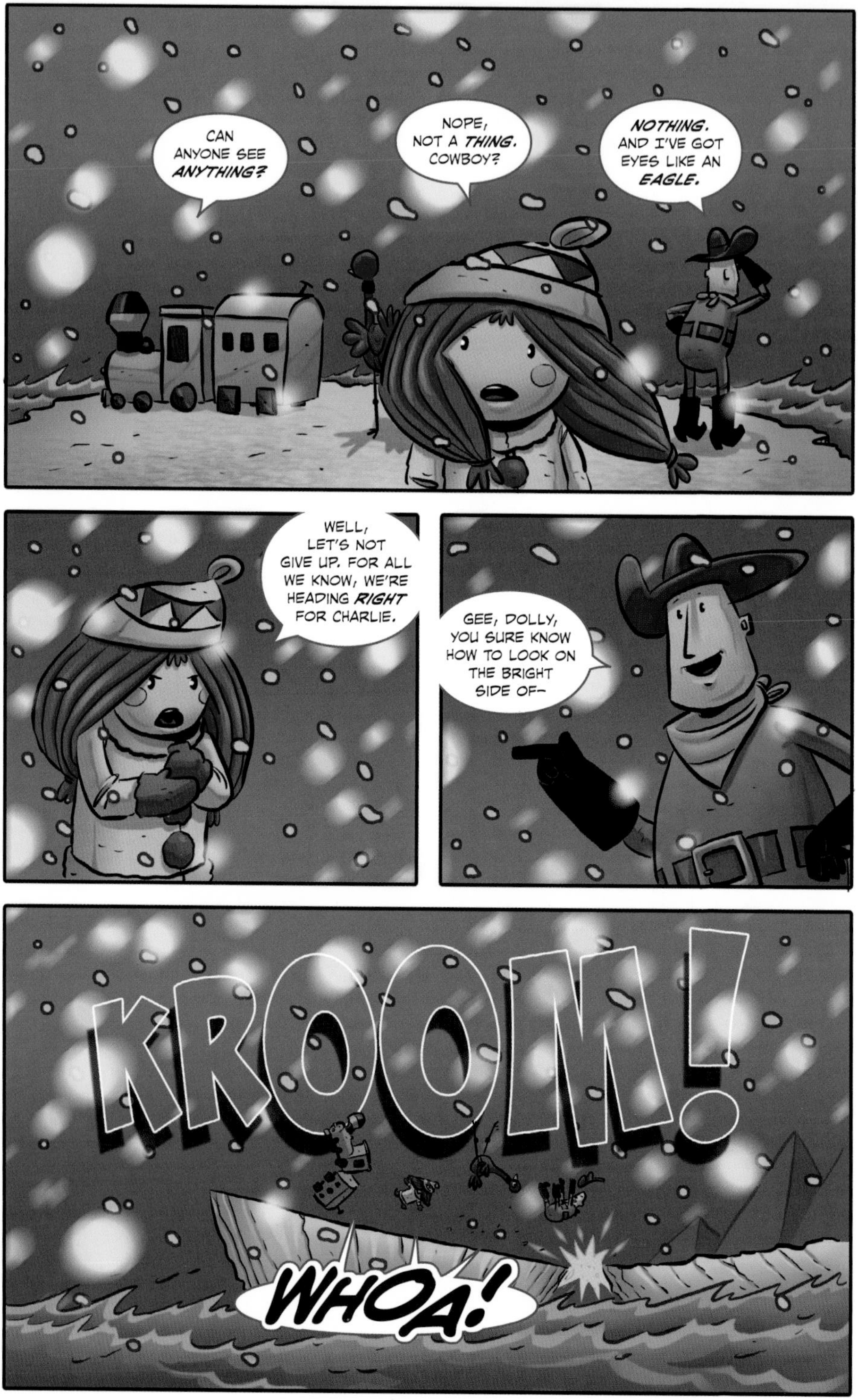
CAN ANYONE SEE ANYTHING?
NOPE, NOT A THING. COWBOY?
NOTHING. AND I'VE GOT EYES LIKE AN EAGLE.
WELL, LET'S NOT GIVE UP. FOR ALL WE KNOW, WE'RE HEADING RIGHT FOR CHARLIE.
GEE, DOLLY, YOU SURE KNOW HOW TO LOOK ON THE BRIGHT SIDE OF–
KROOM!
WHOA!

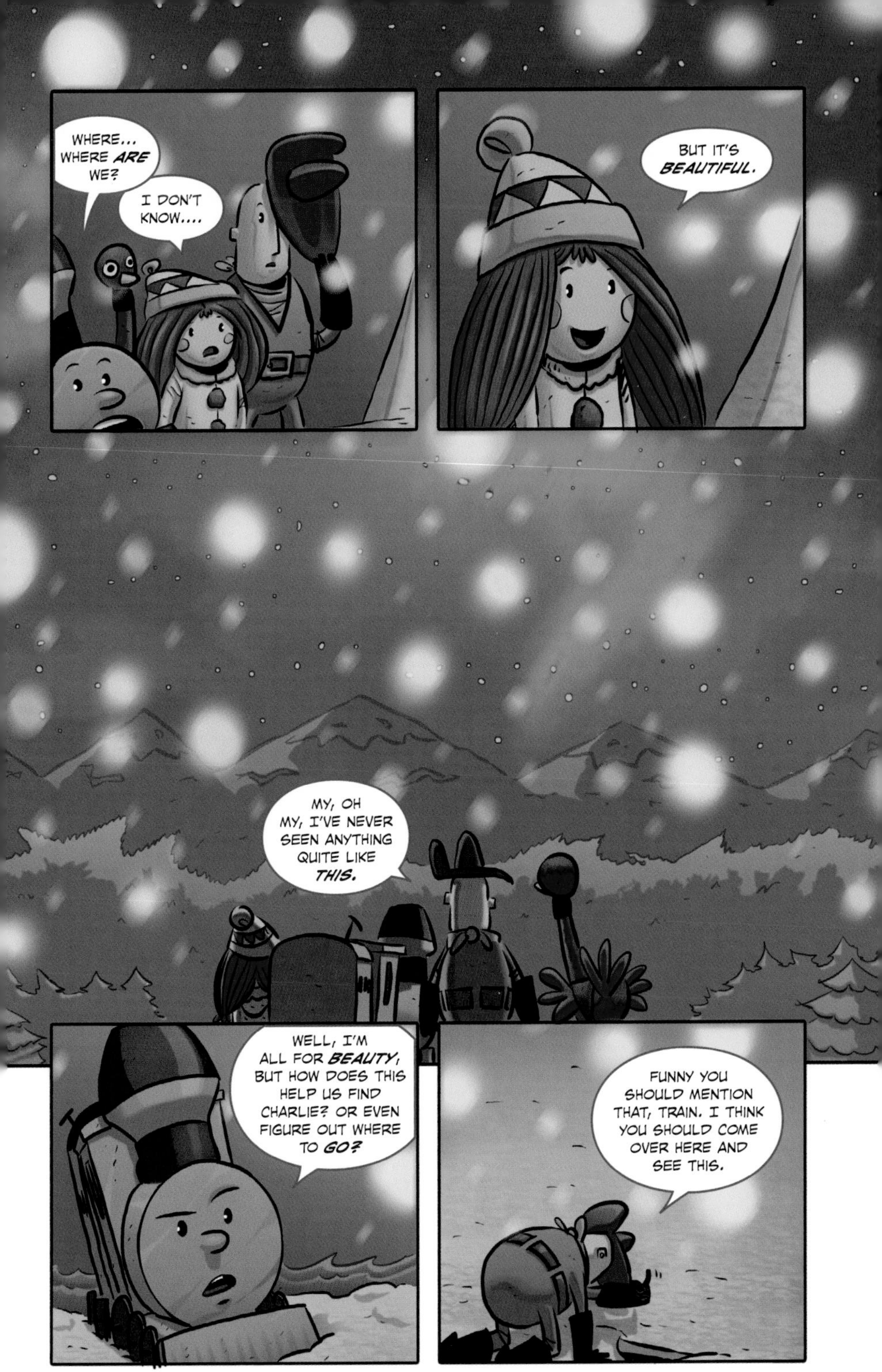
WHERE... WHERE *ARE* WE?
I DON'T KNOW....
BUT IT'S *BEAUTIFUL*.
MY, OH MY, I'VE NEVER SEEN ANYTHING QUITE LIKE *THIS*.
WELL, I'M ALL FOR *BEAUTY*, BUT HOW DOES THIS HELP US FIND CHARLIE? OR EVEN FIGURE OUT WHERE TO *GO?*
FUNNY YOU SHOULD MENTION THAT, TRAIN. I THINK YOU SHOULD COME OVER HERE AND SEE THIS.

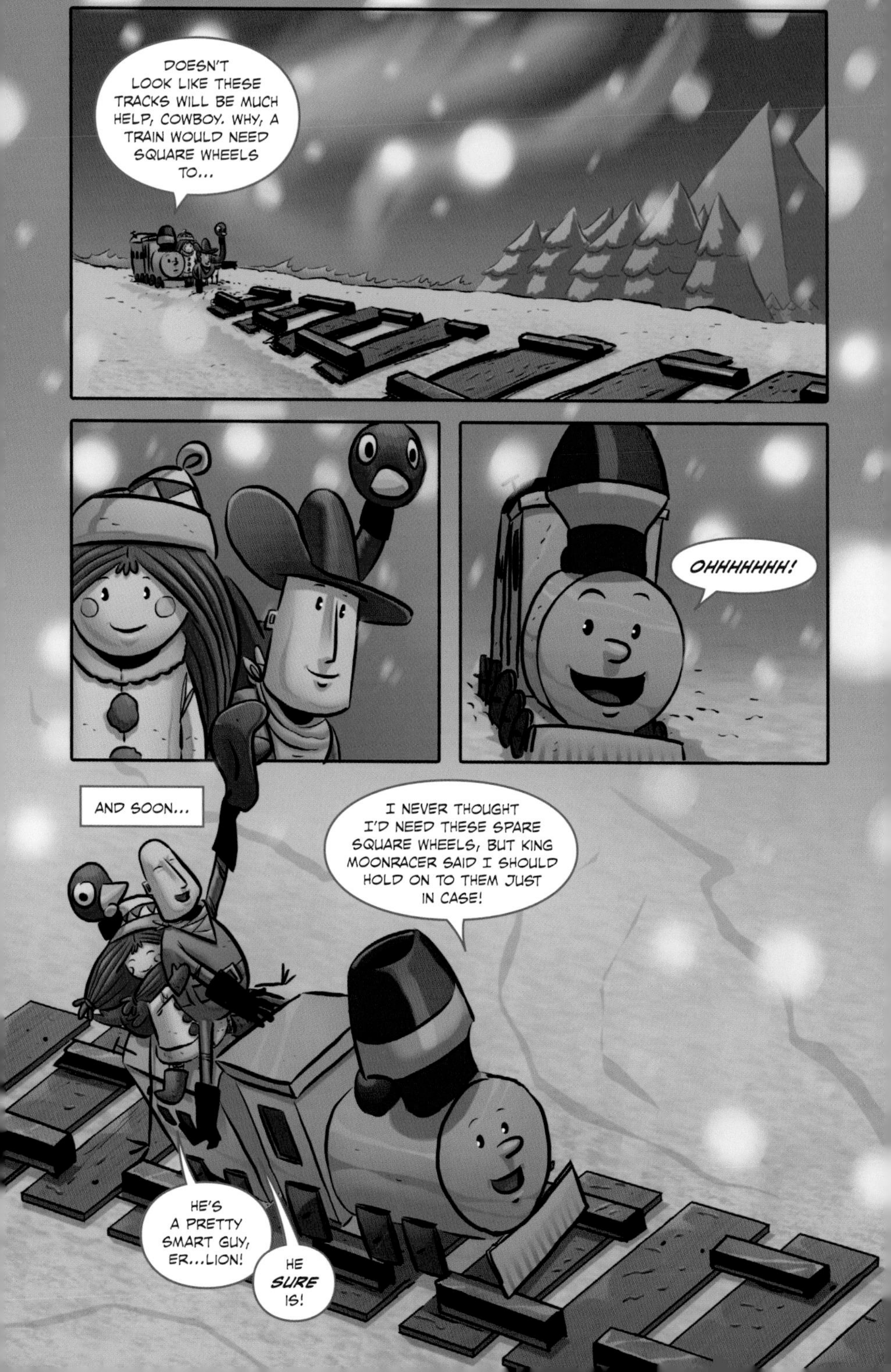
DOESN'T LOOK LIKE THESE TRACKS WILL BE MUCH HELP, COWBOY. WHY, A TRAIN WOULD NEED SQUARE WHEELS TO...
OHHHHHHH!
AND SOON...
I NEVER THOUGHT I'D NEED THESE SPARE SQUARE WHEELS, BUT KING MOONRACER SAID I SHOULD HOLD ON TO THEM JUST IN CASE!
HE'S A PRETTY SMART GUY, ER...LION!
HE *SURE* IS!

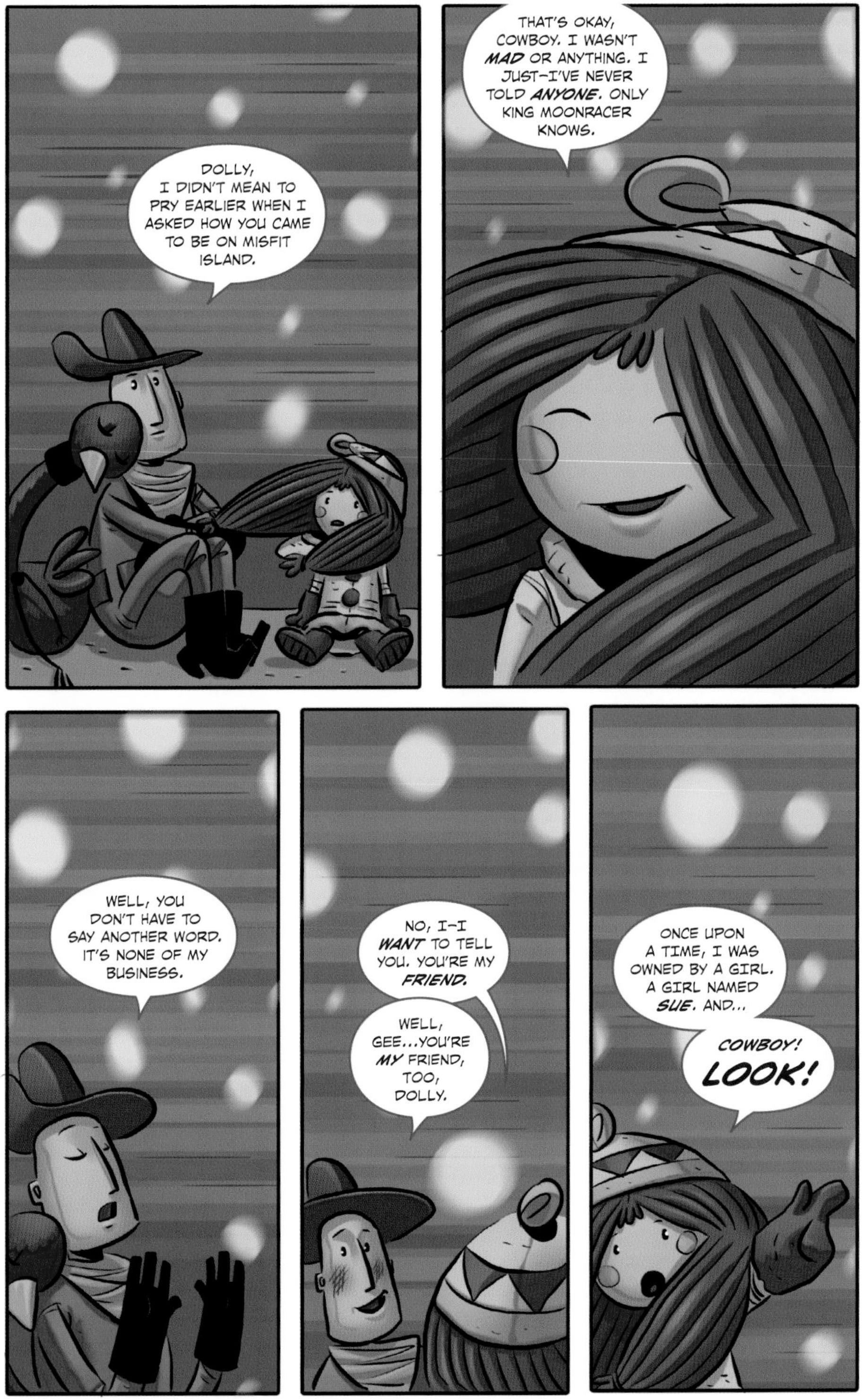
DOLLY, I DIDN'T MEAN TO PRY EARLIER WHEN I ASKED HOW YOU CAME TO BE ON MISFIT ISLAND.
THAT'S OKAY, COWBOY. I WASN'T MAD OR ANYTHING. I JUST—I'VE NEVER TOLD ANYONE. ONLY KING MOONRACER KNOWS.
WELL, YOU DON'T HAVE TO SAY ANOTHER WORD. IT'S NONE OF MY BUSINESS.
NO, I—I WANT TO TELL YOU. YOU'RE MY FRIEND.
WELL, GEE...YOU'RE MY FRIEND, TOO, DOLLY.
ONCE UPON A TIME, I WAS OWNED BY A GIRL. A GIRL NAMED SUE. AND...
COWBOY! LOOK!

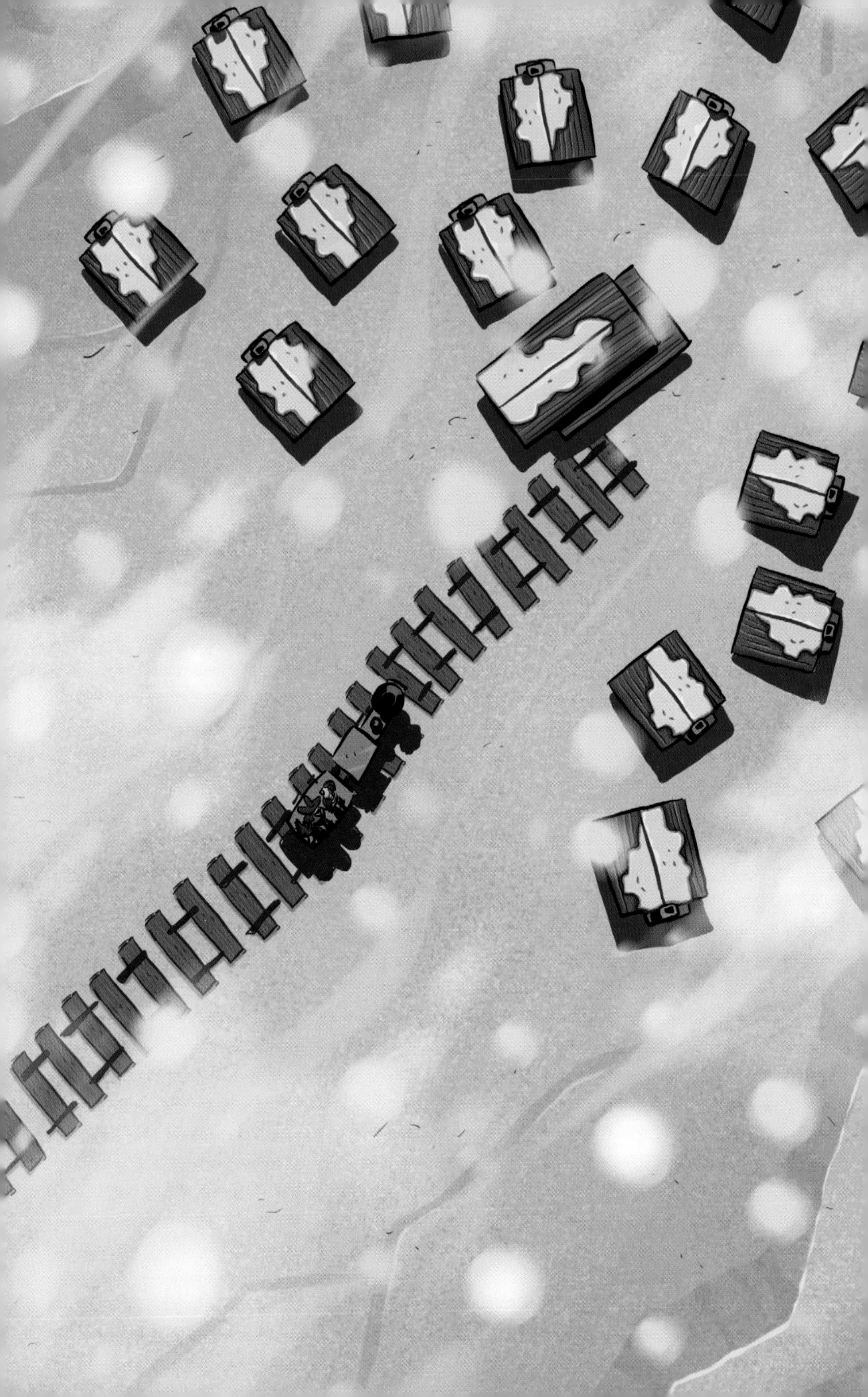

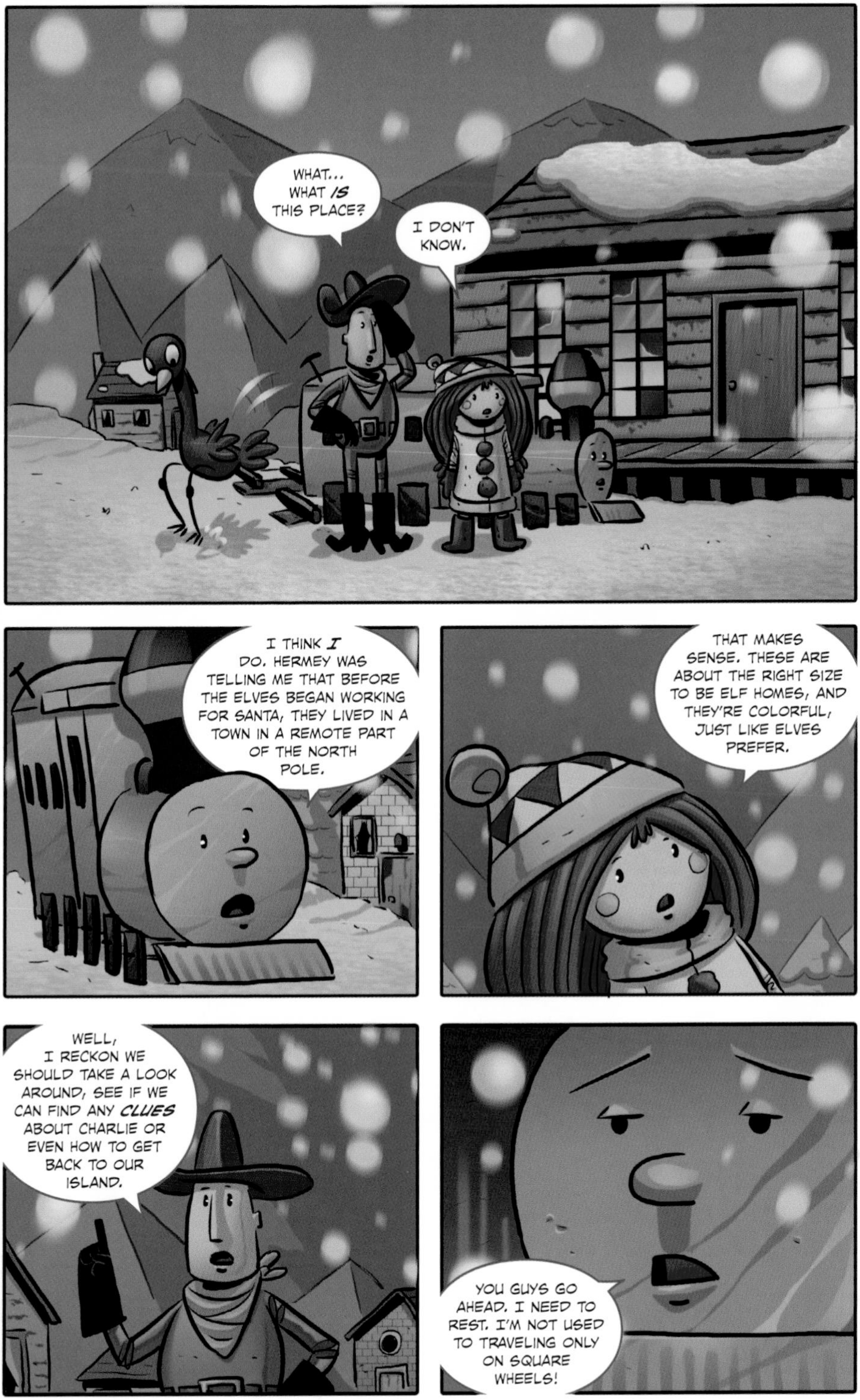
WHAT... WHAT *IS* THIS PLACE?
I DON'T KNOW.
I THINK *I* DO. HERMEY WAS TELLING ME THAT BEFORE THE ELVES BEGAN WORKING FOR SANTA, THEY LIVED IN A TOWN IN A REMOTE PART OF THE NORTH POLE.
THAT MAKES SENSE. THESE ARE ABOUT THE RIGHT SIZE TO BE ELF HOMES, AND THEY'RE COLORFUL, JUST LIKE ELVES PREFER.
WELL, I RECKON WE SHOULD TAKE A LOOK AROUND, SEE IF WE CAN FIND ANY *CLUES* ABOUT CHARLIE OR EVEN HOW TO GET BACK TO OUR ISLAND.
YOU GUYS GO AHEAD. I NEED TO REST. I'M NOT USED TO TRAVELING ONLY ON SQUARE WHEELS!

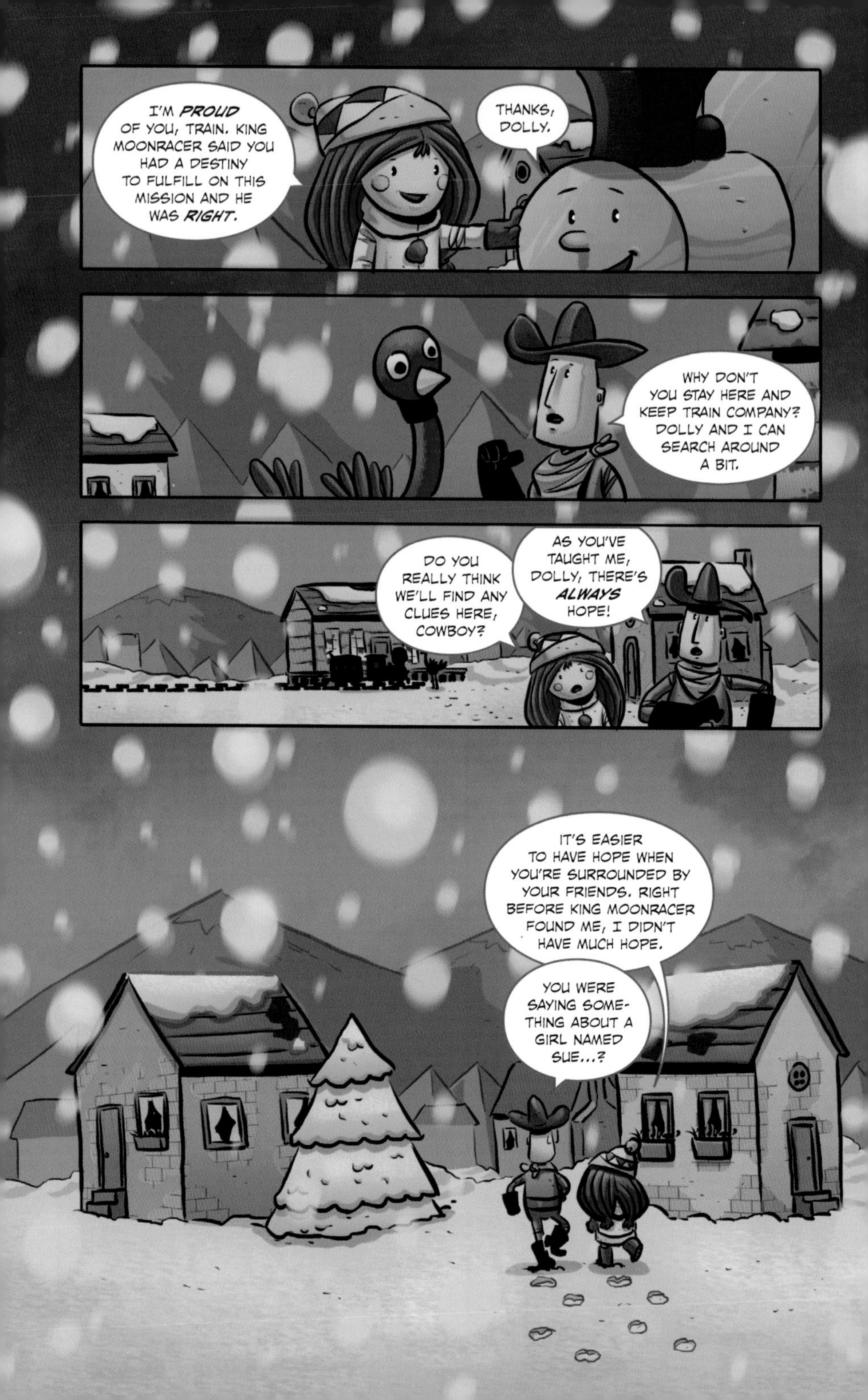
I'M PROUD OF YOU, TRAIN. KING MOONRACER SAID YOU HAD A DESTINY TO FULFILL ON THIS MISSION AND HE WAS RIGHT.
THANKS, DOLLY.
WHY DON'T YOU STAY HERE AND KEEP TRAIN COMPANY? DOLLY AND I CAN SEARCH AROUND A BIT.
DO YOU REALLY THINK WE'LL FIND ANY CLUES HERE, COWBOY?
AS YOU'VE TAUGHT ME, DOLLY, THERE'S ALWAYS HOPE!
IT'S EASIER TO HAVE HOPE WHEN YOU'RE SURROUNDED BY YOUR FRIENDS. RIGHT BEFORE KING MOONRACER FOUND ME, I DIDN'T HAVE MUCH HOPE.
YOU WERE SAYING SOME-THING ABOUT A GIRL NAMED SUE...?

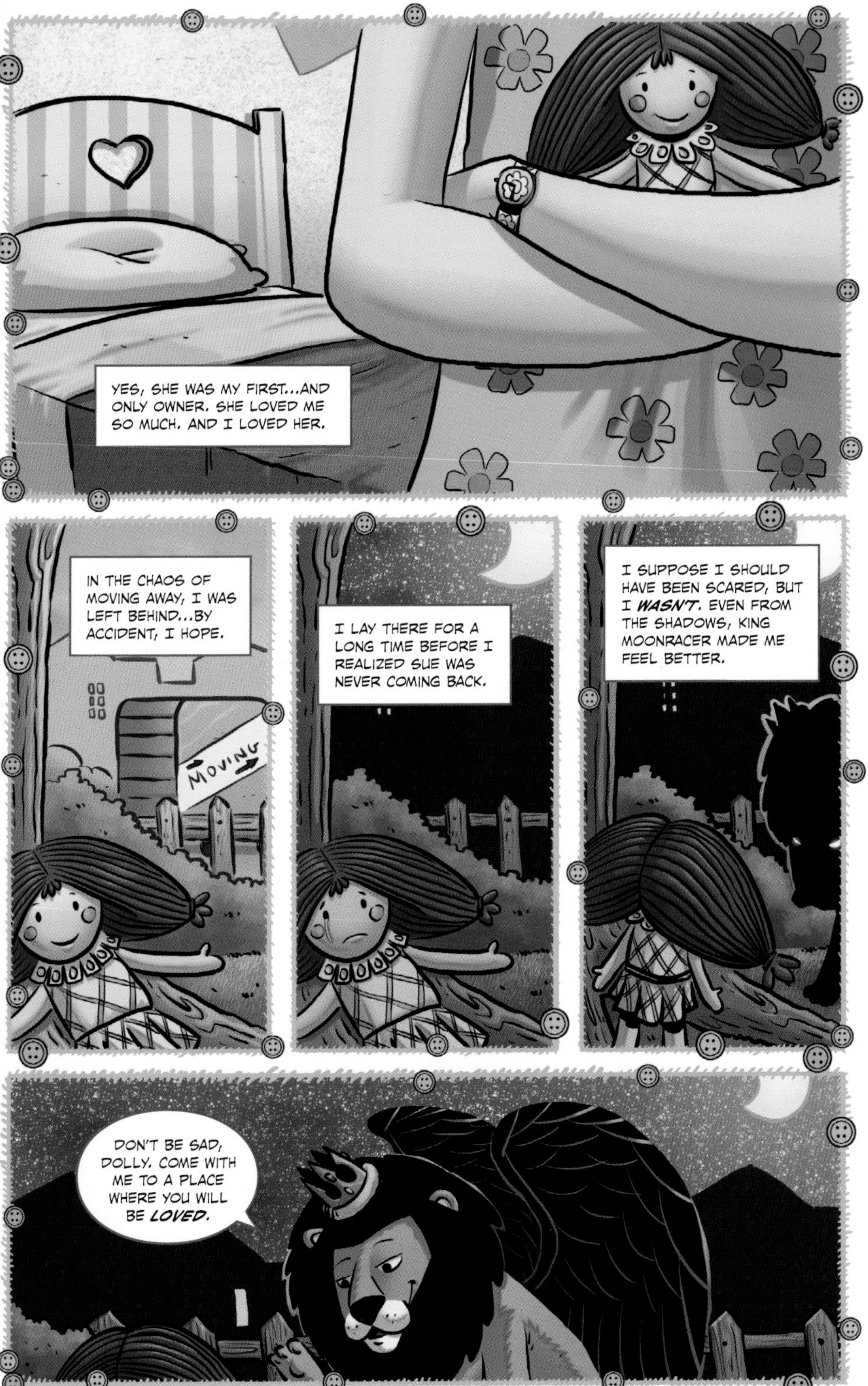
YES, SHE WAS MY FIRST...AND ONLY OWNER. SHE LOVED ME SO MUCH. AND I LOVED HER.
IN THE CHAOS OF MOVING AWAY, I WAS LEFT BEHIND...BY ACCIDENT, I HOPE.
MOVING
I LAY THERE FOR A LONG TIME BEFORE I REALIZED SUE WAS NEVER COMING BACK.
I SUPPOSE I SHOULD HAVE BEEN SCARED, BUT I *WASN'T*. EVEN FROM THE SHADOWS, KING MOONRACER MADE ME FEEL BETTER.
DON'T BE SAD, DOLLY. COME WITH ME TO A PLACE WHERE YOU WILL BE *LOVED*.

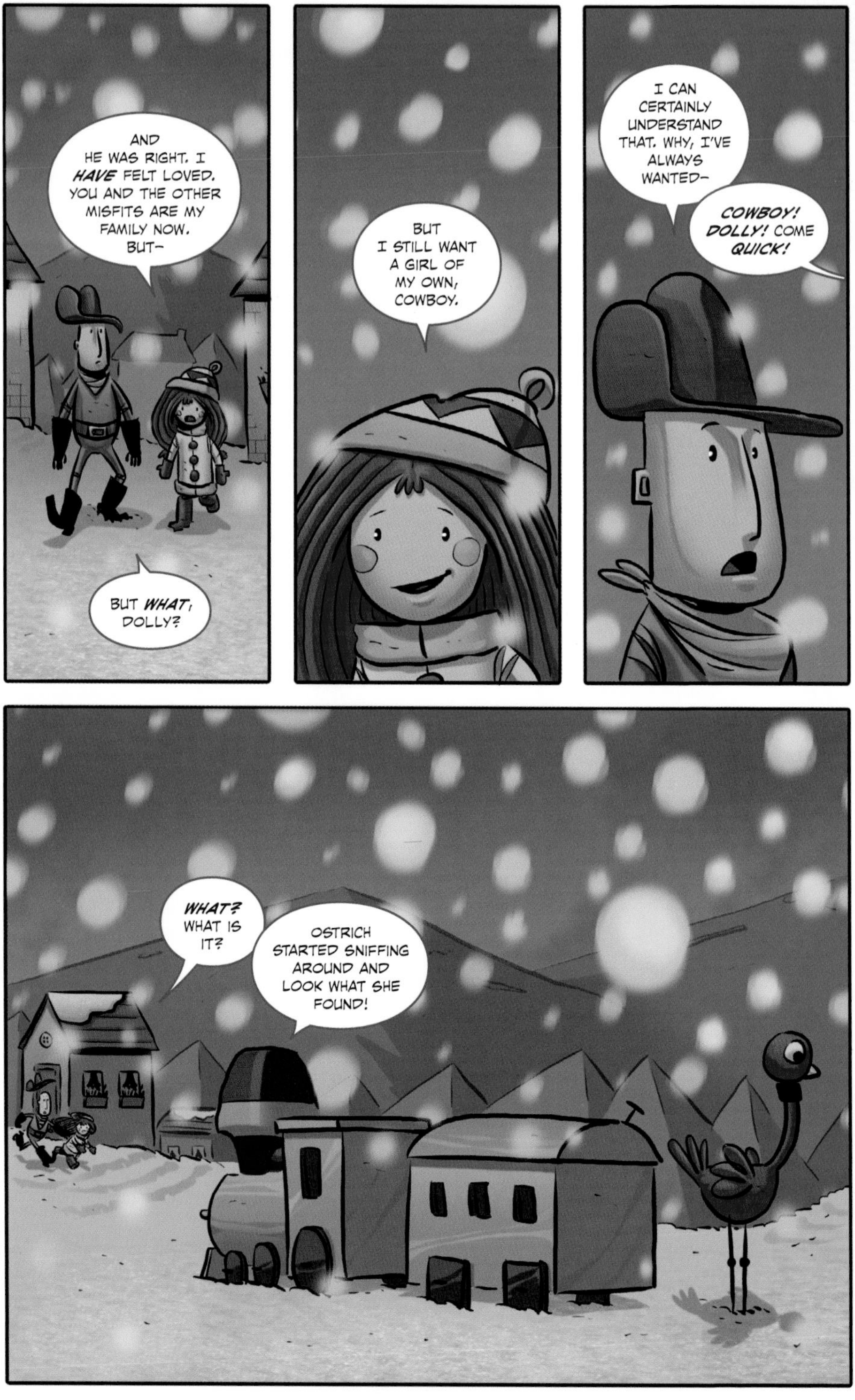
AND HE WAS RIGHT. I *HAVE* FELT LOVED. YOU AND THE OTHER MISFITS ARE MY FAMILY NOW. BUT–
BUT *WHAT*, DOLLY?
BUT I STILL WANT A GIRL OF MY OWN, COWBOY.
I CAN CERTAINLY UNDERSTAND THAT. WHY, I'VE ALWAYS WANTED–
COWBOY! DOLLY! COME *QUICK!*
WHAT? WHAT IS IT?
OSTRICH STARTED SNIFFING AROUND AND LOOK WHAT SHE FOUND!

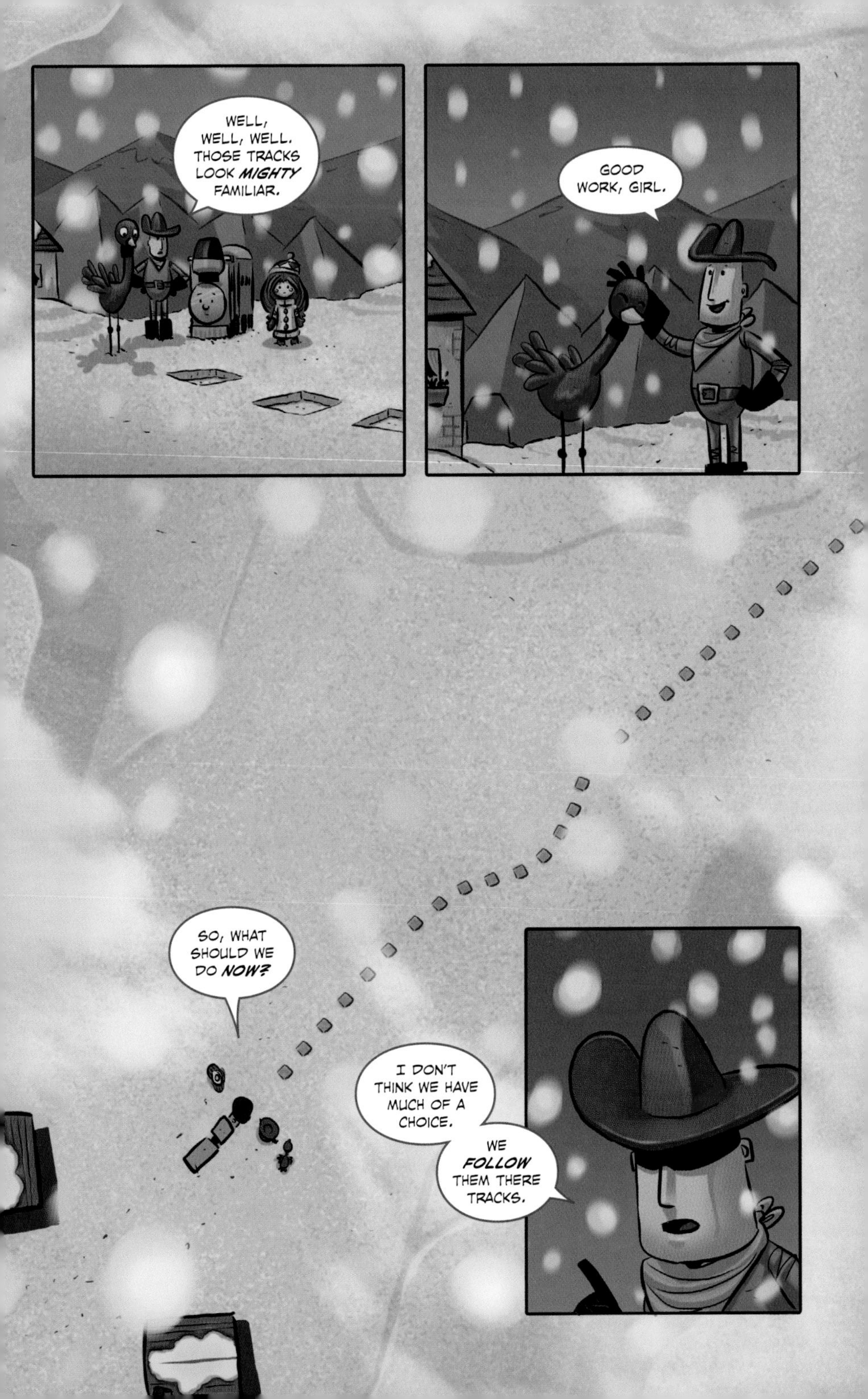
WELL, WELL, WELL. THOSE TRACKS LOOK MIGHTY FAMILIAR.
GOOD WORK, GIRL.
SO, WHAT SHOULD WE DO NOW?
I DON'T THINK WE HAVE MUCH OF A CHOICE.
WE FOLLOW THEM THERE TRACKS.

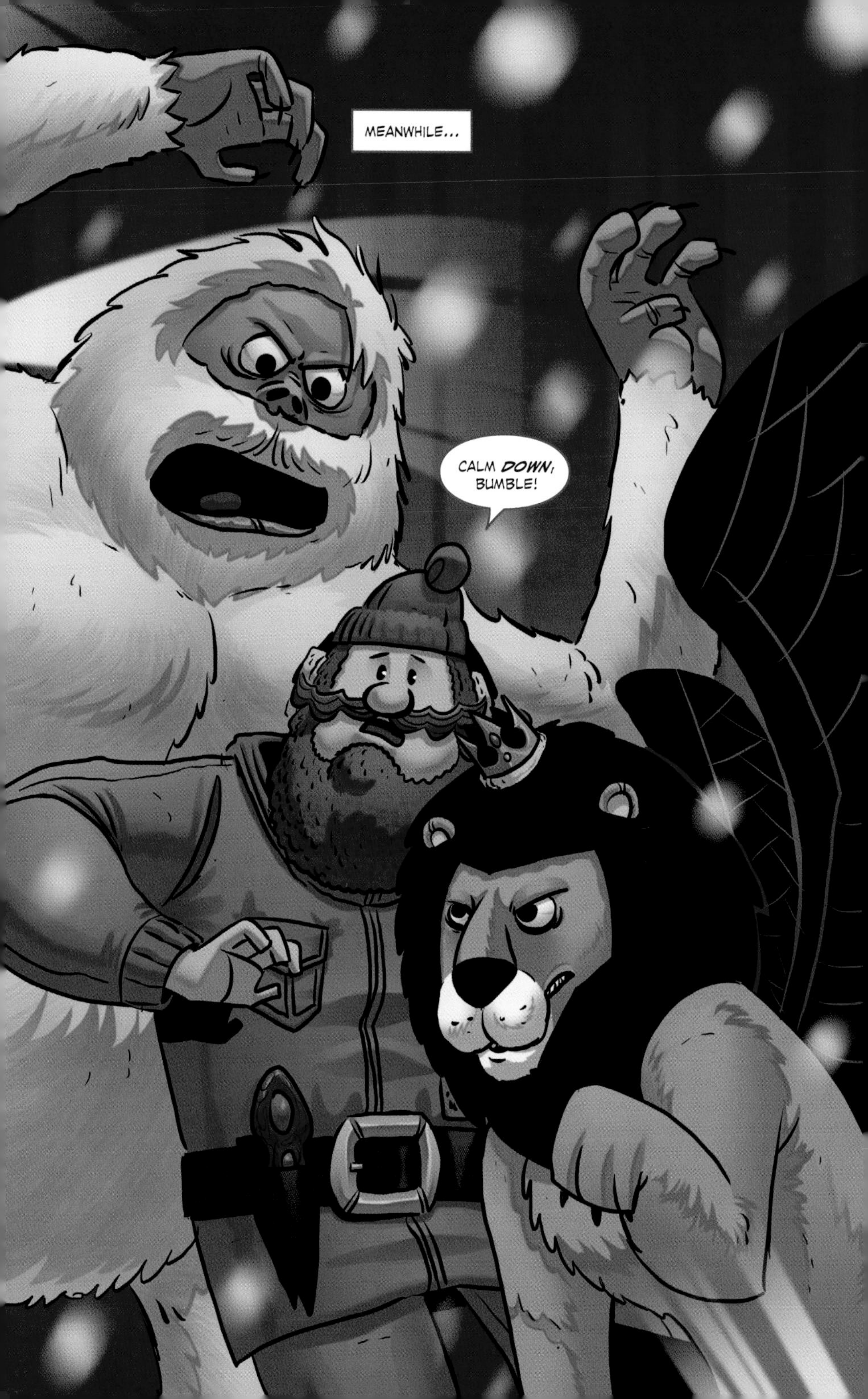
MEANWHILE...
CALM DOWN, BUMBLE!

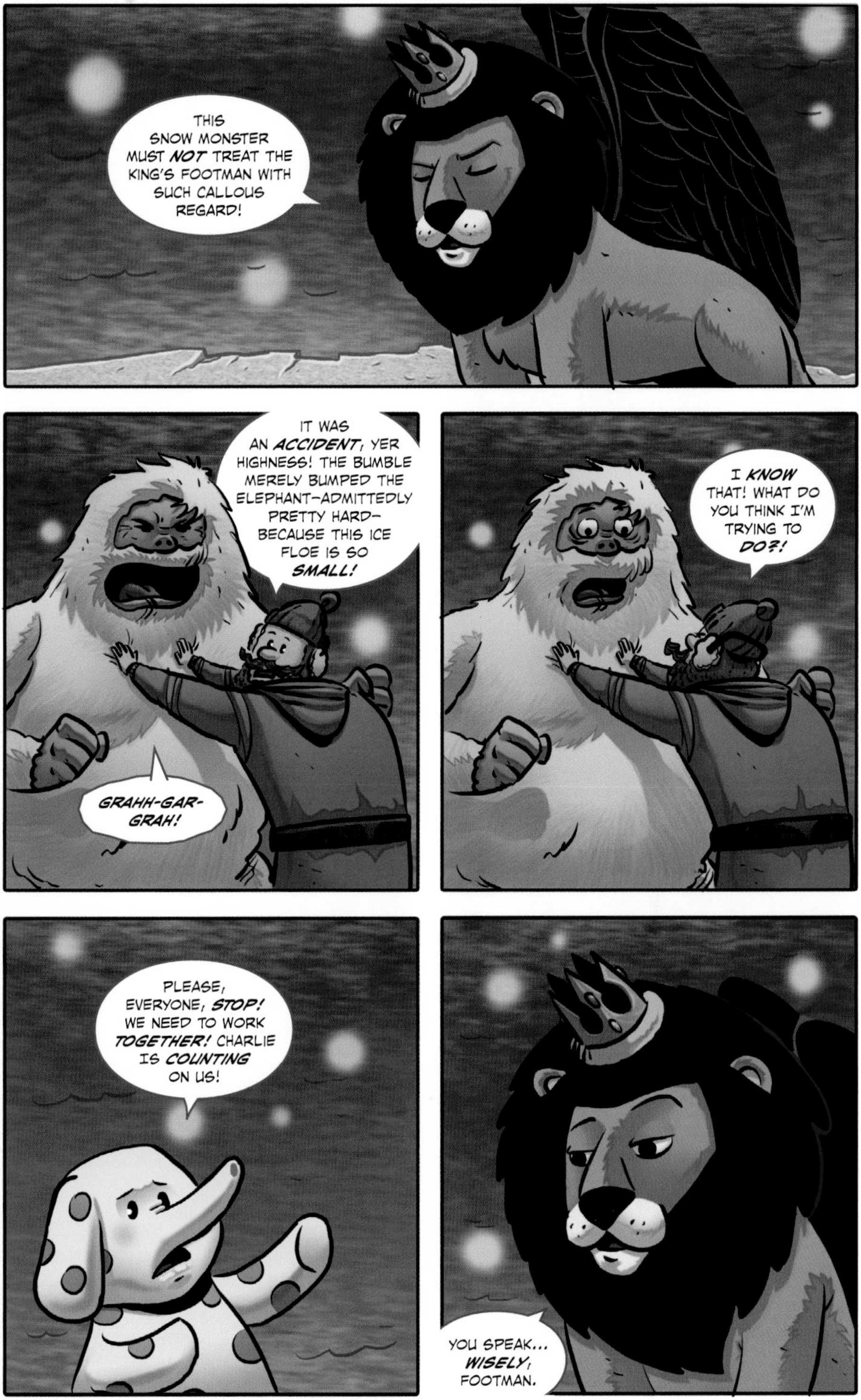
THIS SNOW MONSTER MUST NOT TREAT THE KING'S FOOTMAN WITH SUCH CALLOUS REGARD!
IT WAS AN ACCIDENT, YER HIGHNESS! THE BUMBLE MERELY BUMPED THE ELEPHANT—ADMITTEDLY PRETTY HARD—BECAUSE THIS ICE FLOE IS SO SMALL!
GRAHH-GAR-GRAH!
I KNOW THAT! WHAT DO YOU THINK I'M TRYING TO DO?!
PLEASE, EVERYONE, STOP! WE NEED TO WORK TOGETHER! CHARLIE IS COUNTING ON US!
YOU SPEAK... WISELY, FOOTMAN.

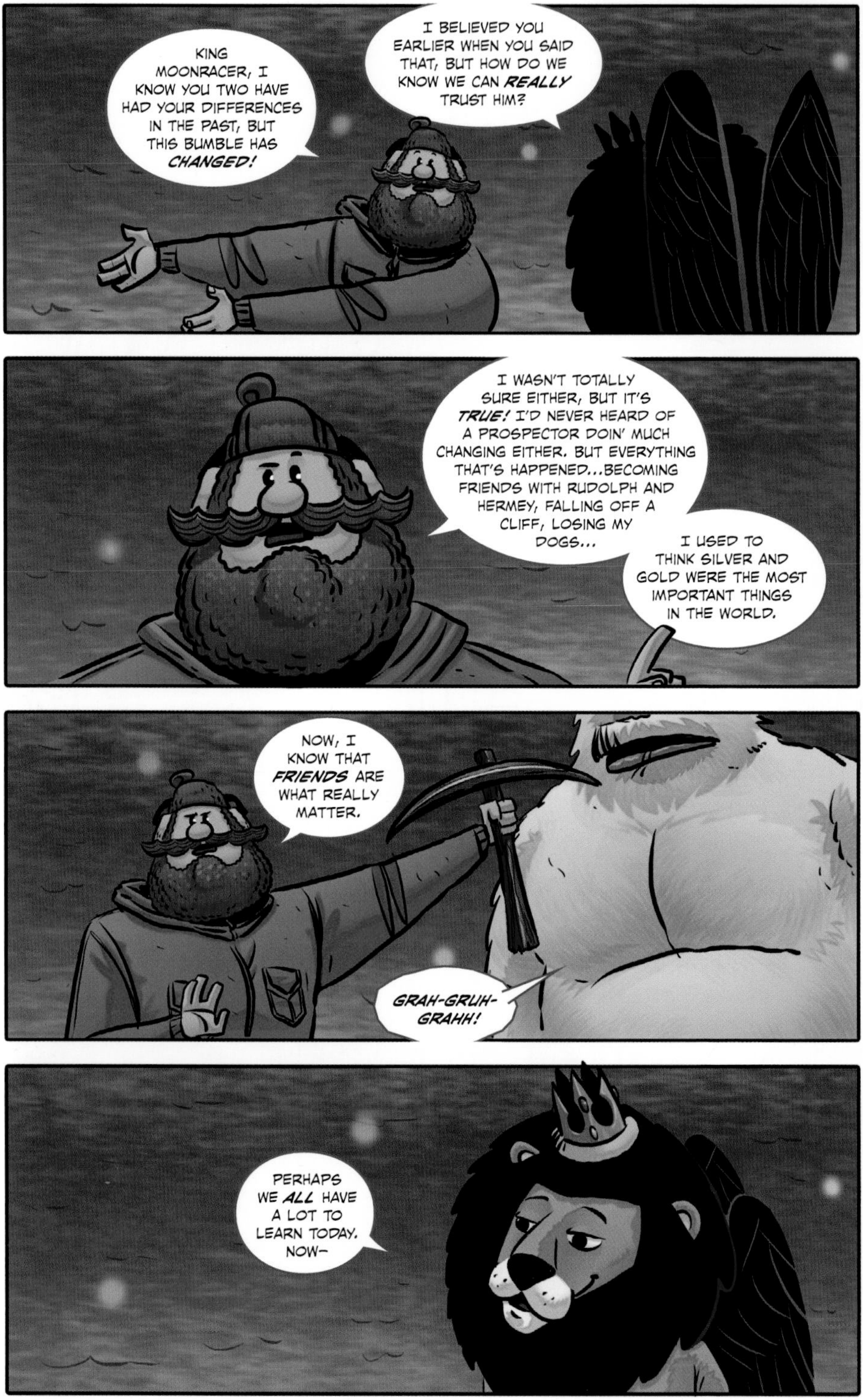
KING MOONRACER, I KNOW YOU TWO HAVE HAD YOUR DIFFERENCES IN THE PAST, BUT THIS BUMBLE HAS *CHANGED!*
I BELIEVED YOU EARLIER WHEN YOU SAID THAT, BUT HOW DO WE KNOW WE CAN *REALLY* TRUST HIM?
I WASN'T TOTALLY SURE EITHER, BUT IT'S *TRUE!* I'D NEVER HEARD OF A PROSPECTOR DOIN' MUCH CHANGING EITHER. BUT EVERYTHING THAT'S HAPPENED...BECOMING FRIENDS WITH RUDOLPH AND HERMEY, FALLING OFF A CLIFF, LOSING MY DOGS...
I USED TO THINK SILVER AND GOLD WERE THE MOST IMPORTANT THINGS IN THE WORLD.
NOW, I KNOW THAT *FRIENDS* ARE WHAT REALLY MATTER.
GRAH-GRUH-GRAHH!
PERHAPS WE *ALL* HAVE A LOT TO LEARN TODAY. NOW–

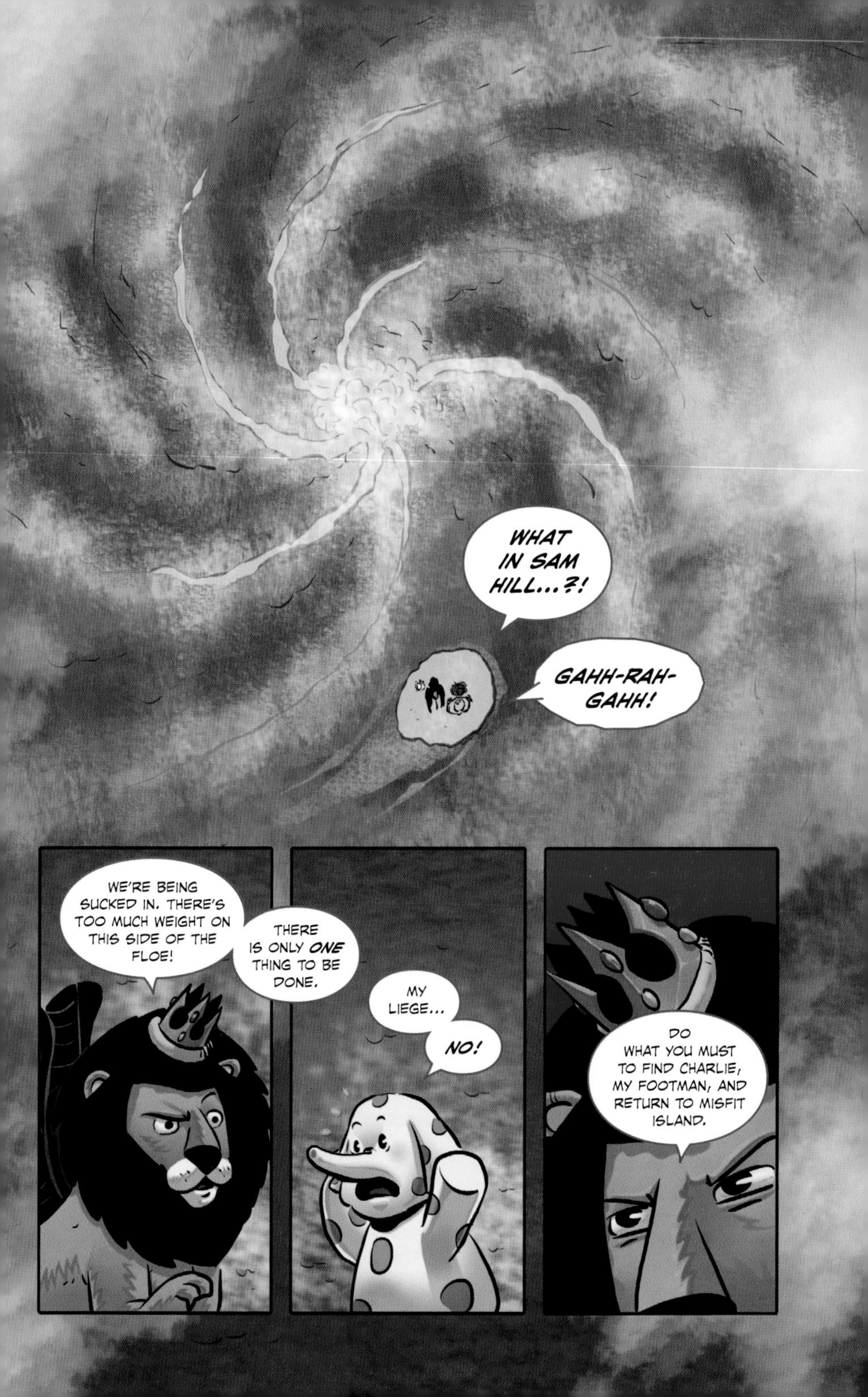
WHAT IN SAM HILL...?!
GAHH-RAH-GAHH!
WE'RE BEING SUCKED IN. THERE'S TOO MUCH WEIGHT ON THIS SIDE OF THE FLOE!
THERE IS ONLY *ONE* THING TO BE DONE.
MY LIEGE...
NO!
DO WHAT YOU MUST TO FIND CHARLIE, MY FOOTMAN, AND RETURN TO MISFIT ISLAND.

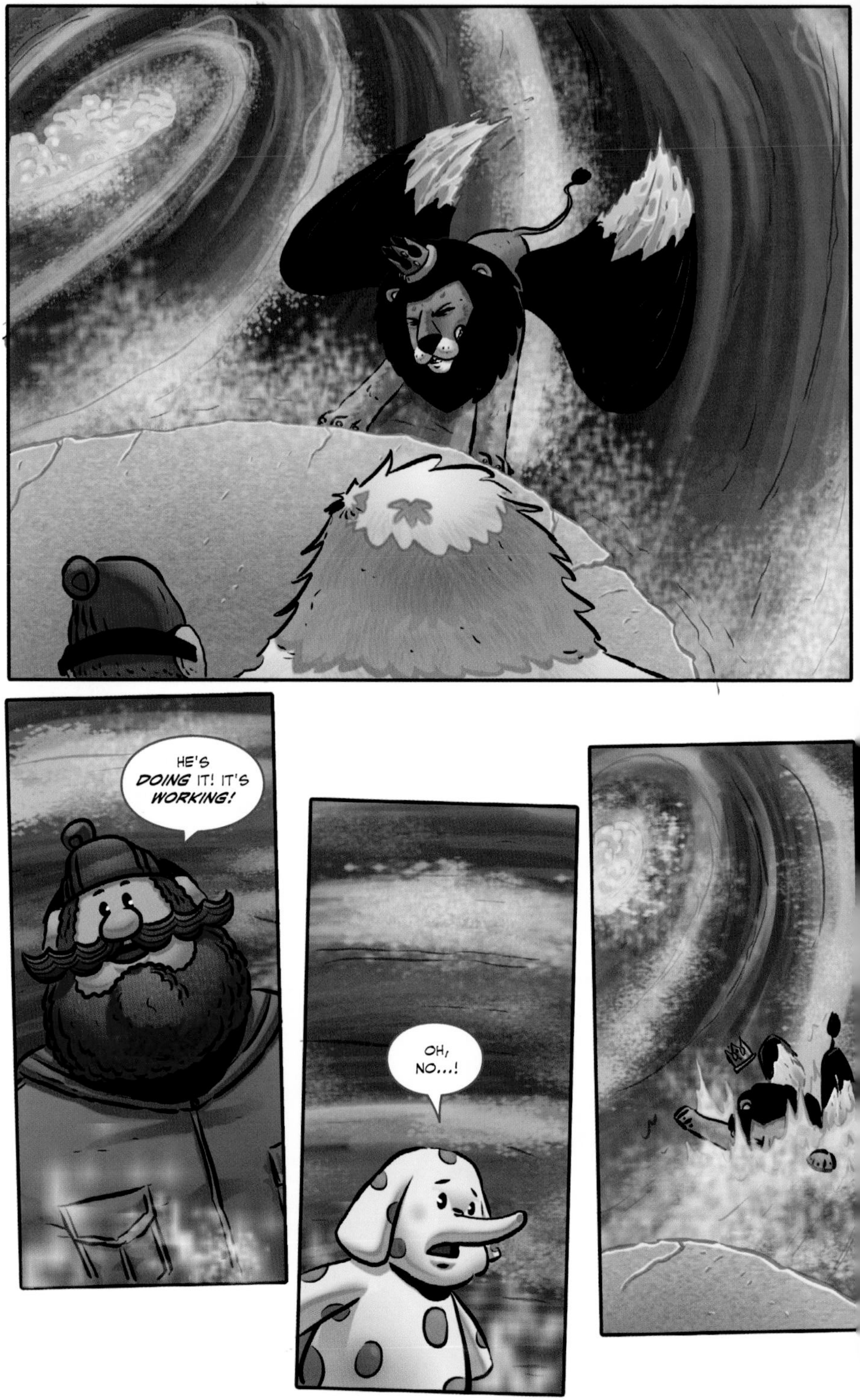
HE'S *DOING* IT! IT'S *WORKING!*
OH, NO...!

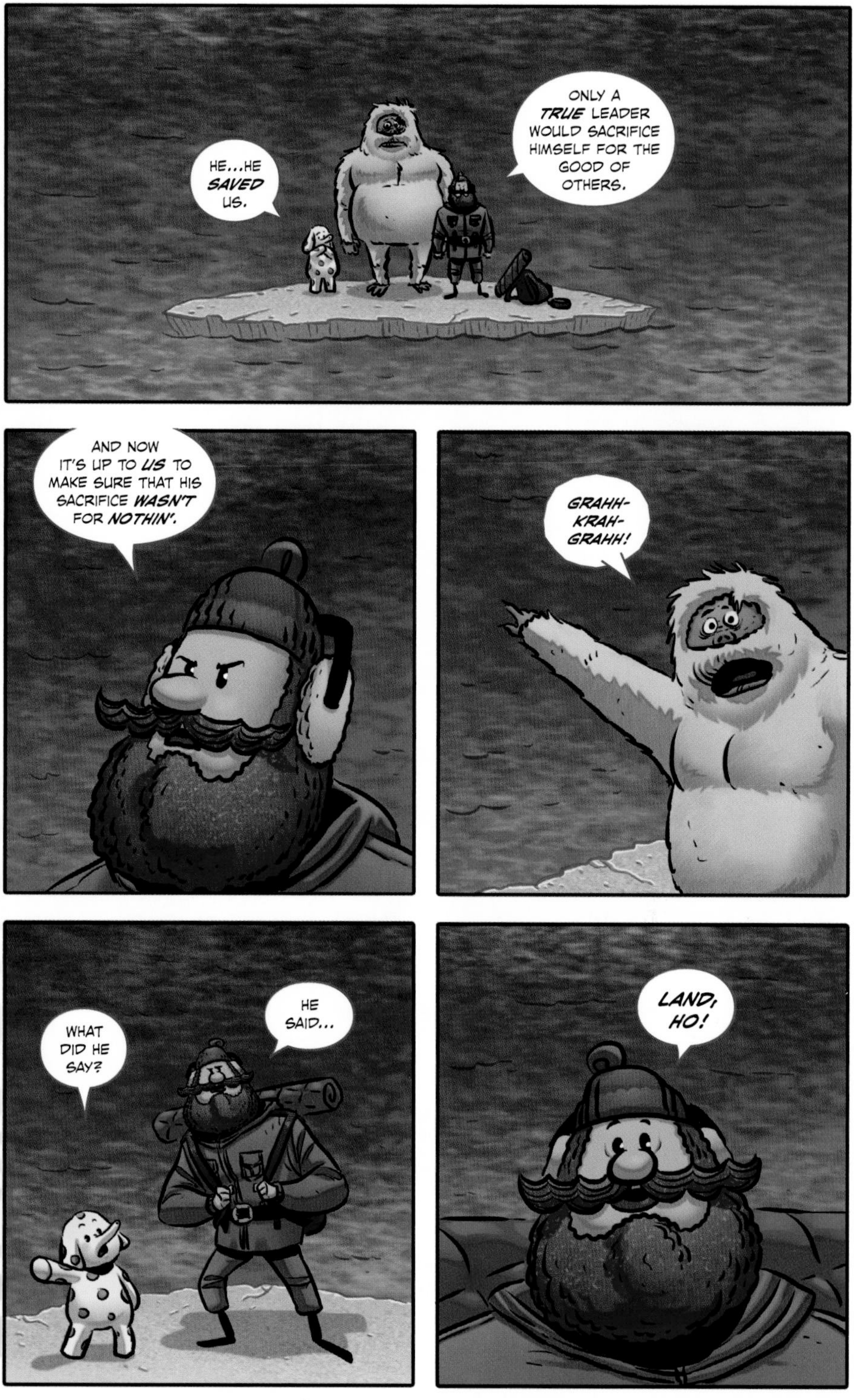
HE...HE SAVED US.
ONLY A TRUE LEADER WOULD SACRIFICE HIMSELF FOR THE GOOD OF OTHERS.
AND NOW IT'S UP TO US TO MAKE SURE THAT HIS SACRIFICE WASN'T FOR NOTHIN'.
GRAHH-KRAH-GRAHH!
WHAT DID HE SAY?
HE SAID...
LAND, HO!

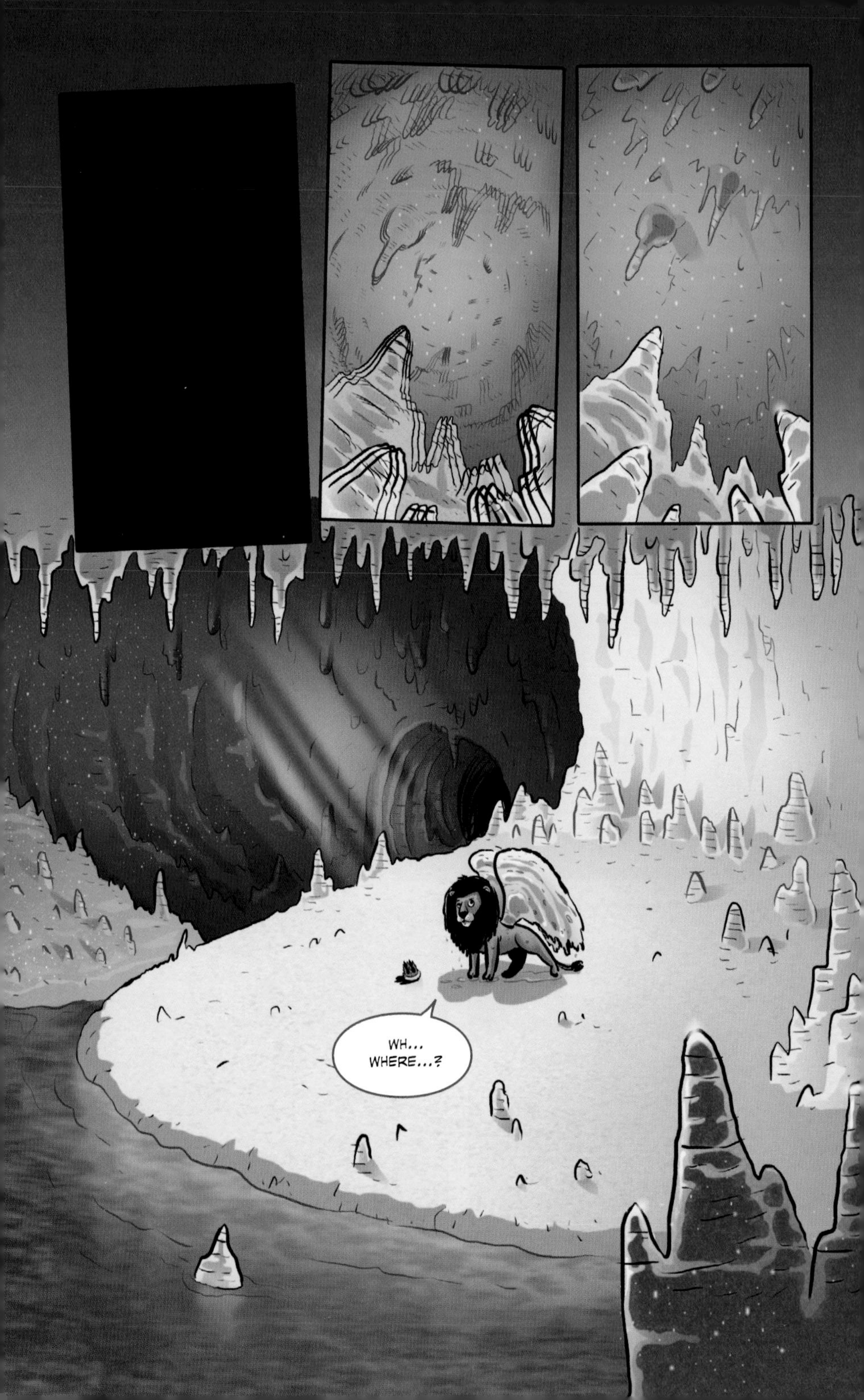
WH...
WHERE...?

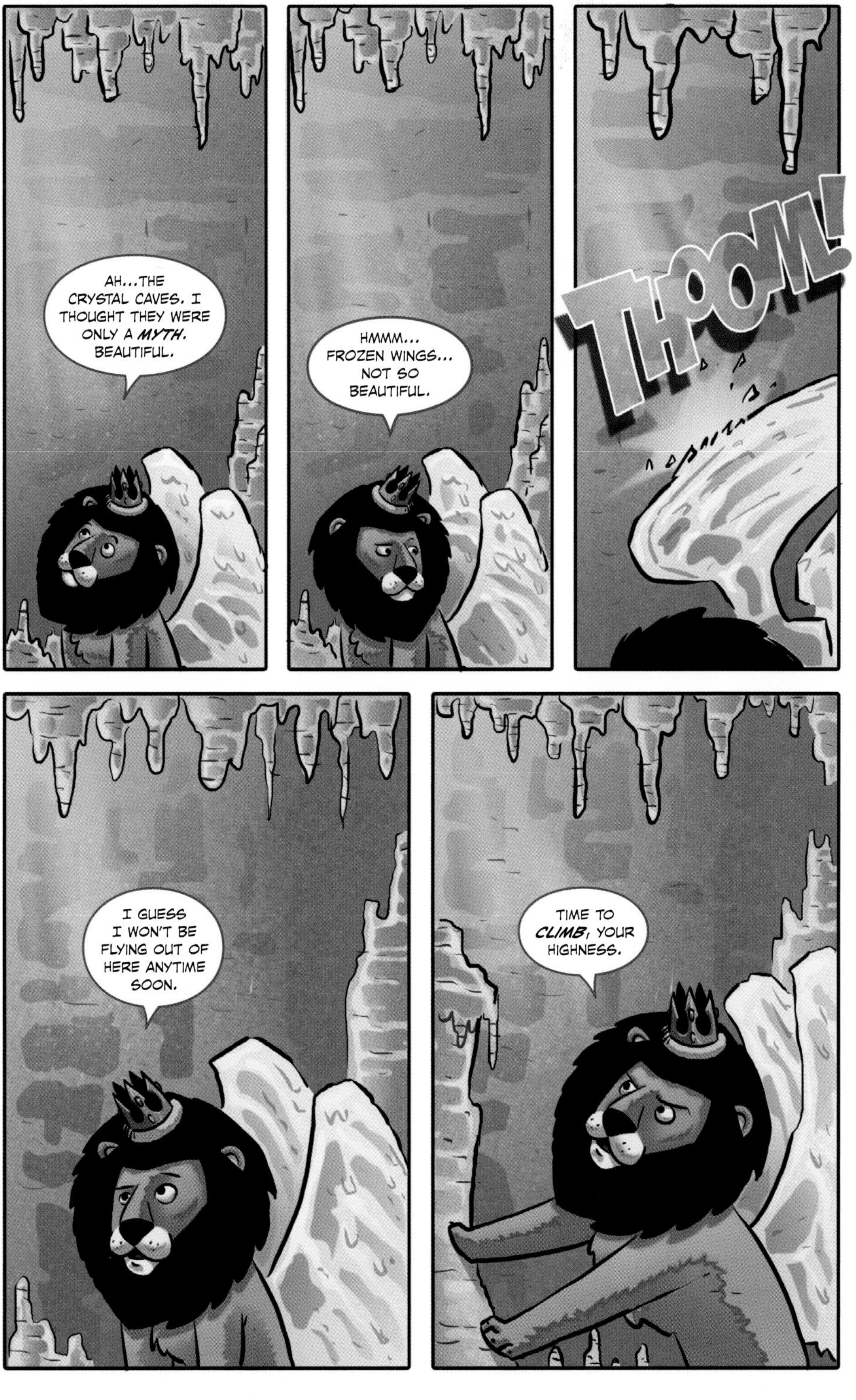
AH...THE CRYSTAL CAVES. I THOUGHT THEY WERE ONLY A MYTH. BEAUTIFUL.
HMMM... FROZEN WINGS... NOT SO BEAUTIFUL.
THOOM!
I GUESS I WON'T BE FLYING OUT OF HERE ANYTIME SOON.
TIME TO CLIMB, YOUR HIGHNESS.

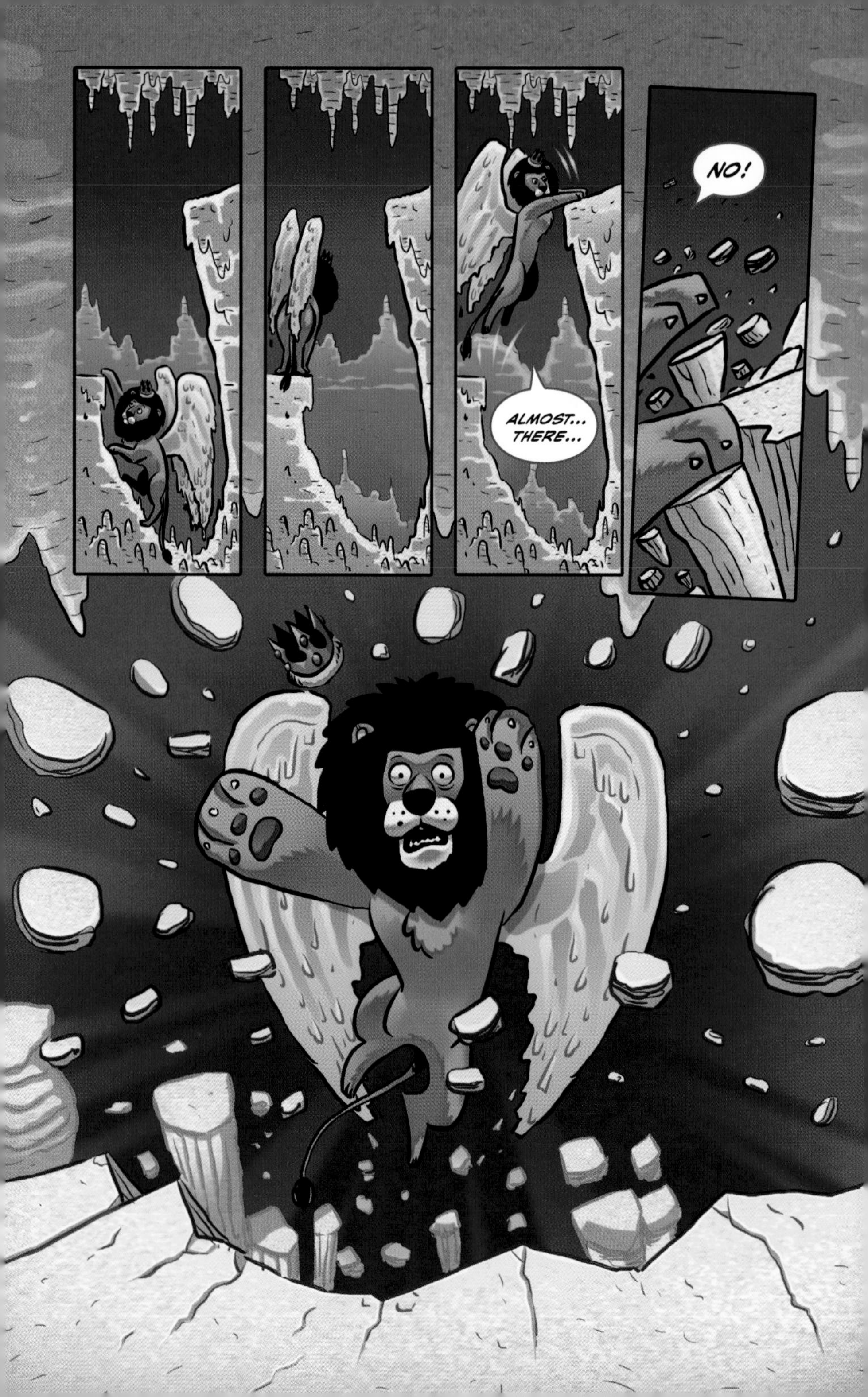
ALMOST... THERE...
NO!

CHAPTER FOUR

LOST AND FOUND

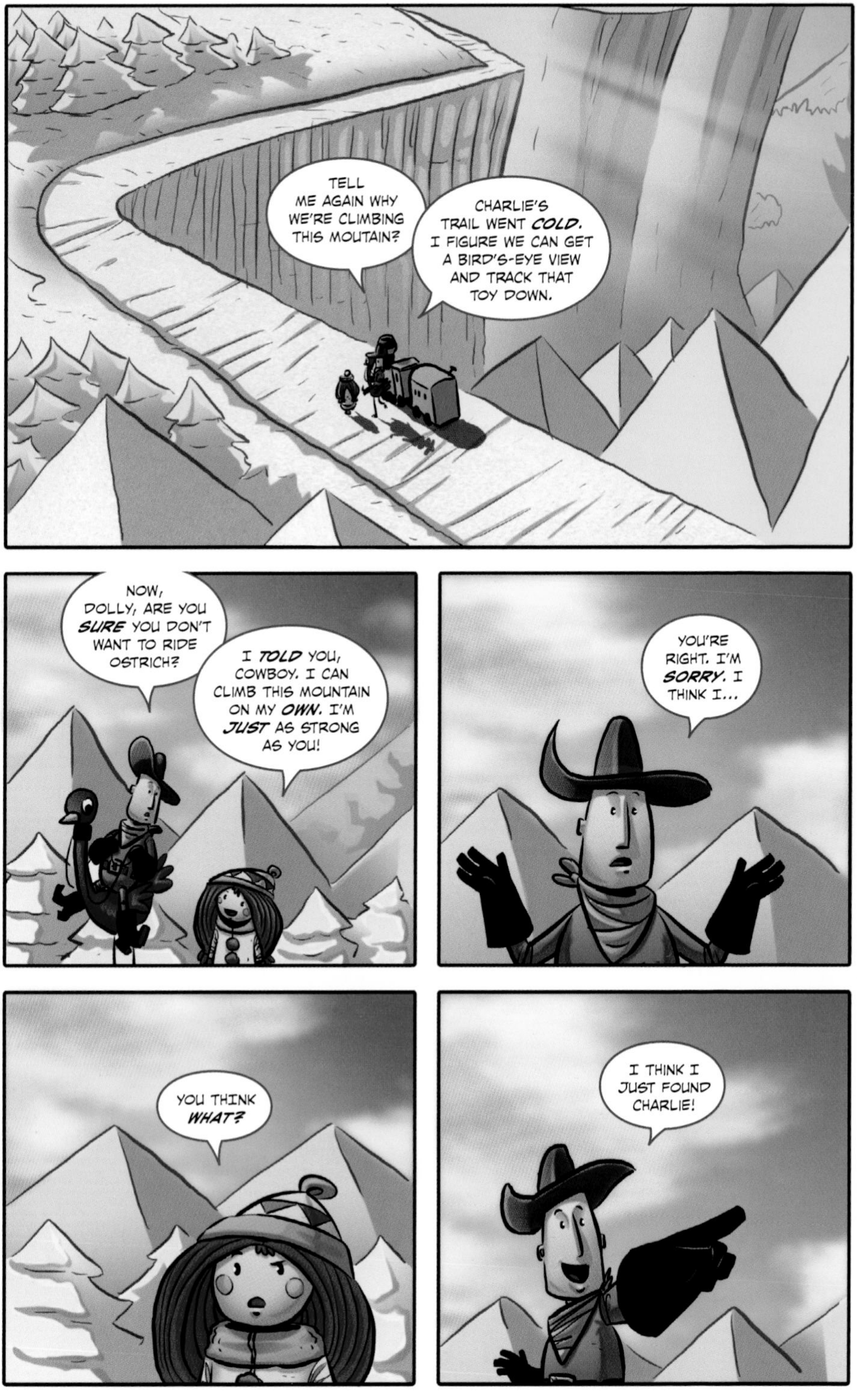
TELL ME AGAIN WHY WE'RE CLIMBING THIS MOUTAIN?
CHARLIE'S TRAIL WENT COLD. I FIGURE WE CAN GET A BIRD'S-EYE VIEW AND TRACK THAT TOY DOWN.
NOW, DOLLY, ARE YOU SURE YOU DON'T WANT TO RIDE OSTRICH?
I TOLD YOU, COWBOY. I CAN CLIMB THIS MOUNTAIN ON MY OWN. I'M JUST AS STRONG AS YOU!
YOU'RE RIGHT. I'M SORRY. I THINK I...
YOU THINK WHAT?
I THINK I JUST FOUND CHARLIE!

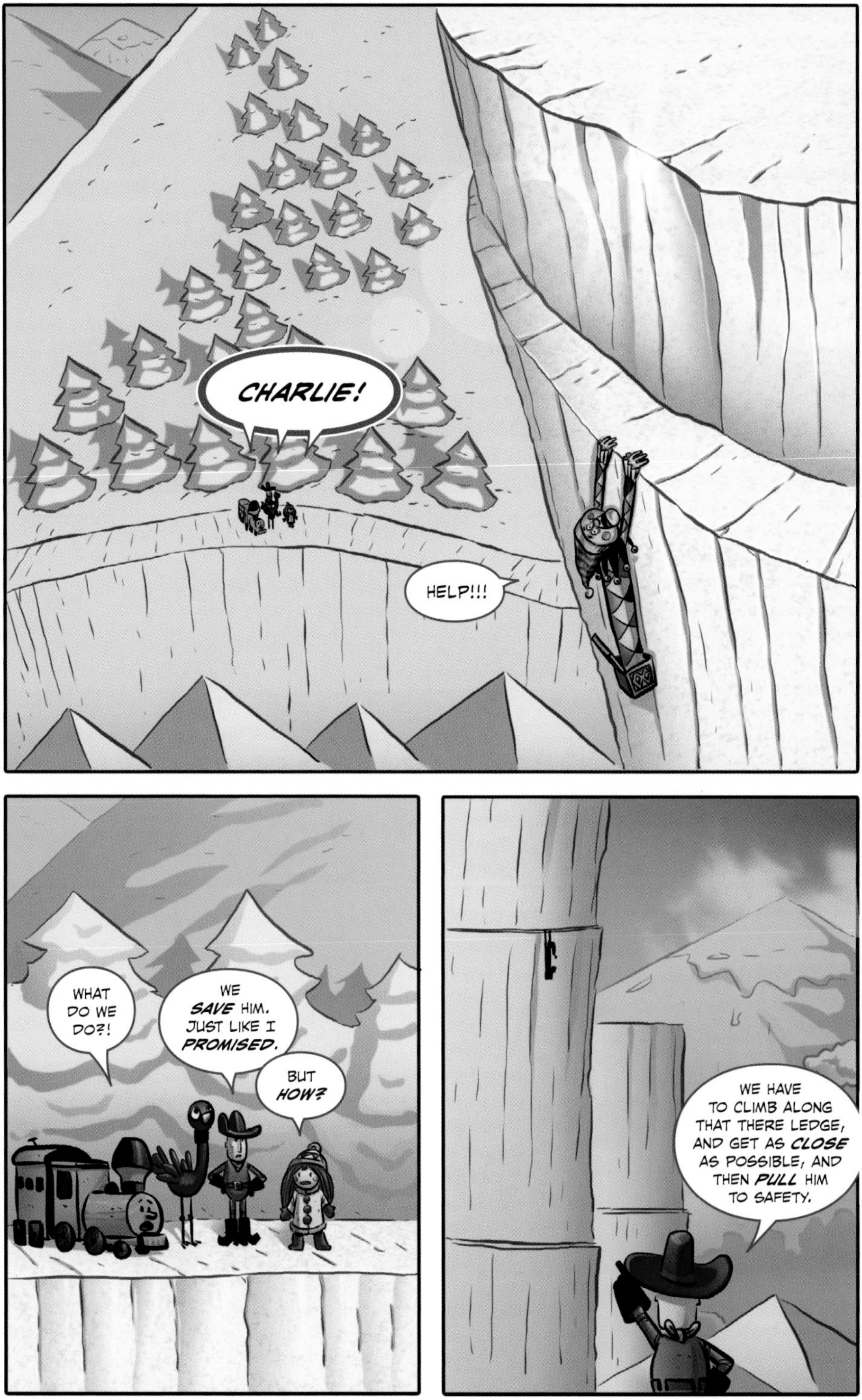
CHARLIE!
HELP!!!
WHAT DO WE DO?!
WE SAVE HIM. JUST LIKE I PROMISED.
BUT HOW?
WE HAVE TO CLIMB ALONG THAT THERE LEDGE, AND GET AS CLOSE AS POSSIBLE, AND THEN PULL HIM TO SAFETY.

BUT THAT LEDGE IS *TINY!* HOW ARE WE SUPPOSED TO FIT?

"WE" WON'T...

BUT *I* WILL.

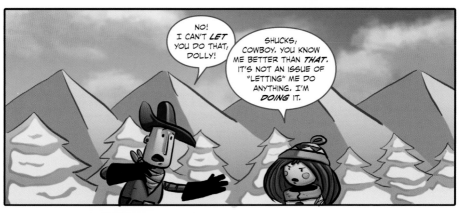

NO! I CAN'T *LET* YOU DO THAT, DOLLY!

SHUCKS, COWBOY. YOU KNOW ME BETTER THAN *THAT.* IT'S NOT AN ISSUE OF "LETTING" ME DO ANYTHING. I'M *DOING* IT.

FINE. YOU'RE RIGHT. JUST BE *CAREFUL* OUT THERE.

I PROMISE. AND YOU *BETTER* NOT FOLLOW ME.

I WON'T.

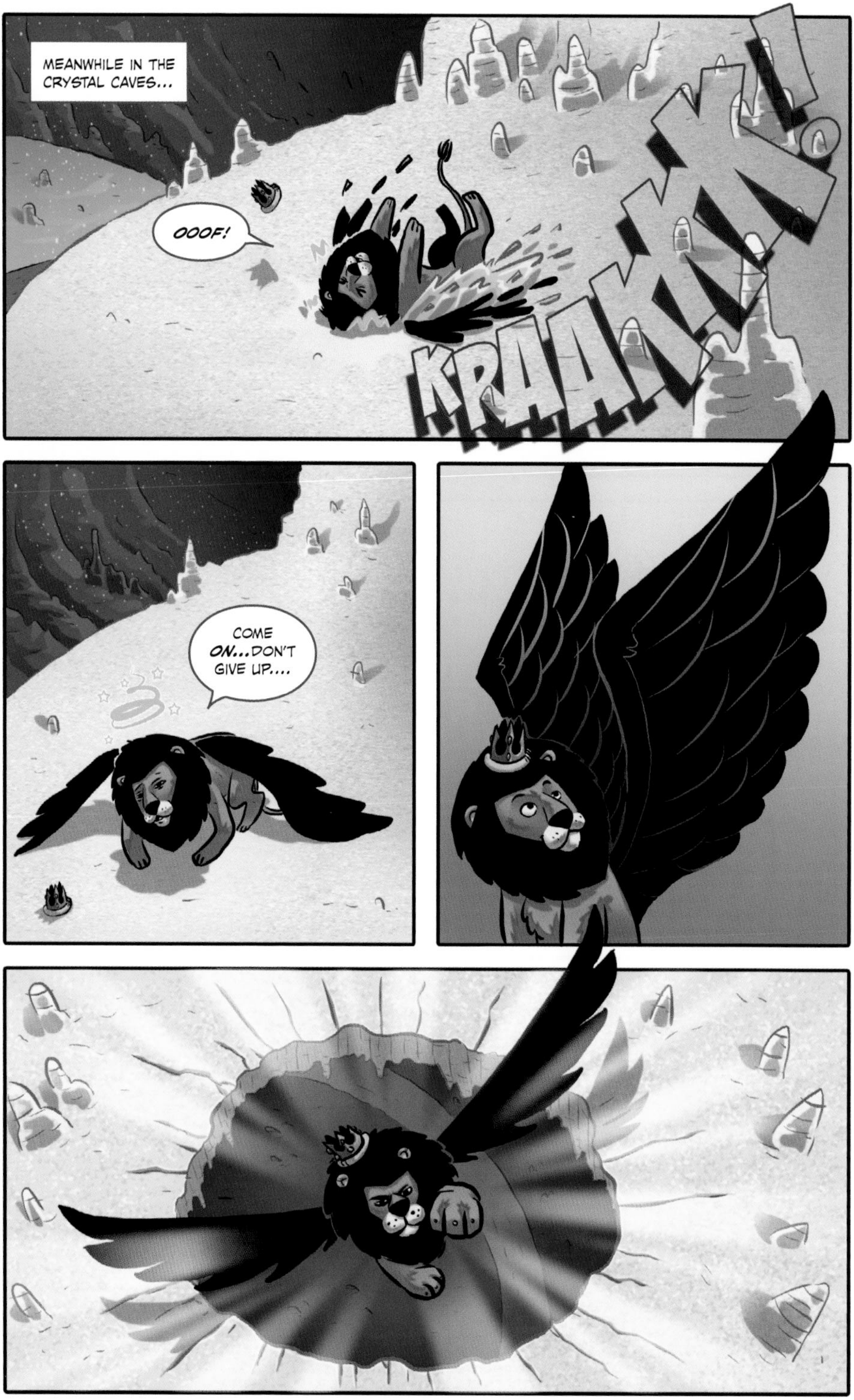
MEANWHILE IN THE CRYSTAL CAVES...
OOOF!
KRAAKKK!
COME ON...DON'T GIVE UP....

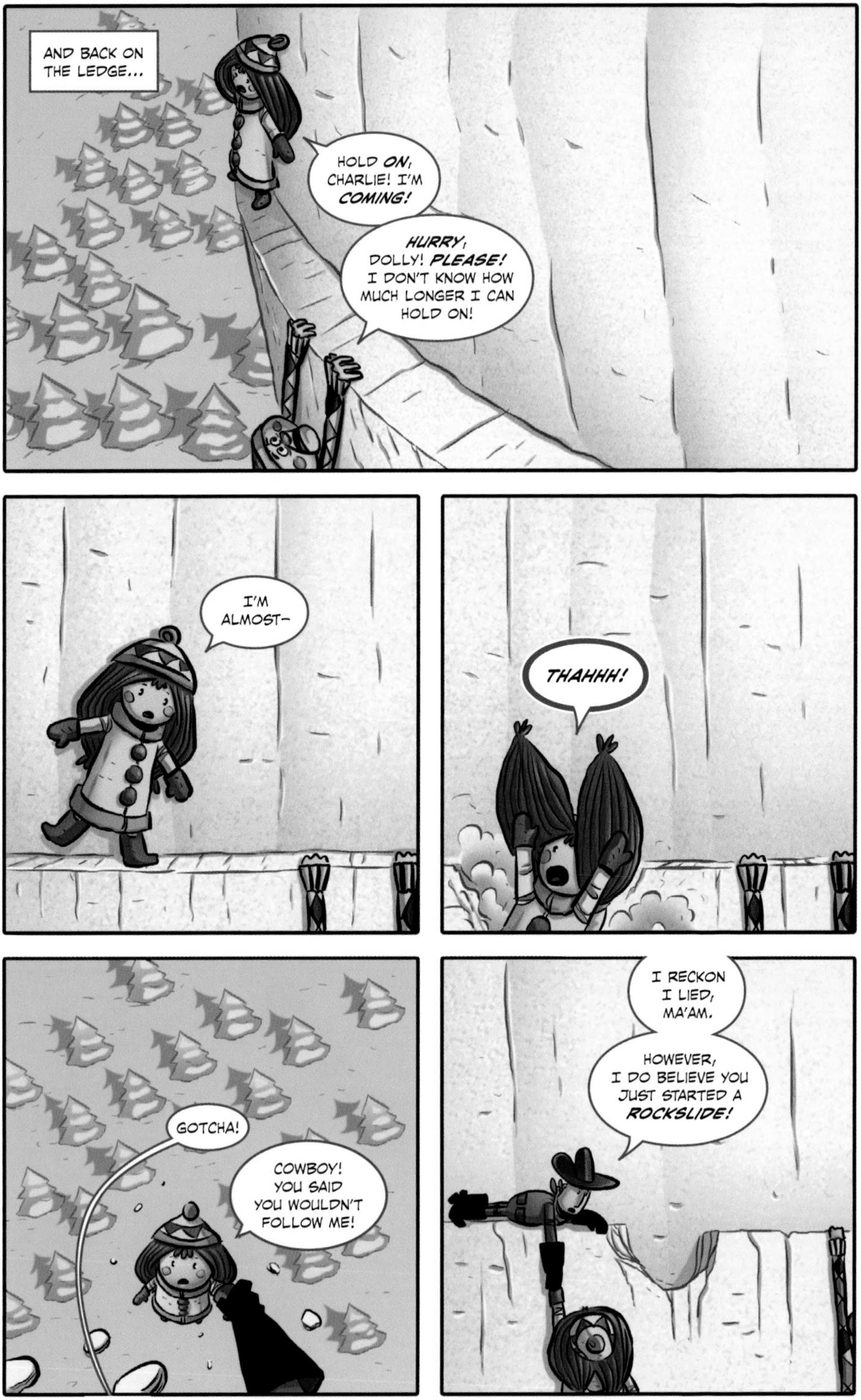
AND BACK ON THE LEDGE...
HOLD ON, CHARLIE! I'M COMING!
HURRY, DOLLY! PLEASE! I DON'T KNOW HOW MUCH LONGER I CAN HOLD ON!
I'M ALMOST-
THAHHH!
GOTCHA!
COWBOY! YOU SAID YOU WOULDN'T FOLLOW ME!
I RECKON I LIED, MA'AM.
HOWEVER, I DO BELIEVE YOU JUST STARTED A ROCKSLIDE!

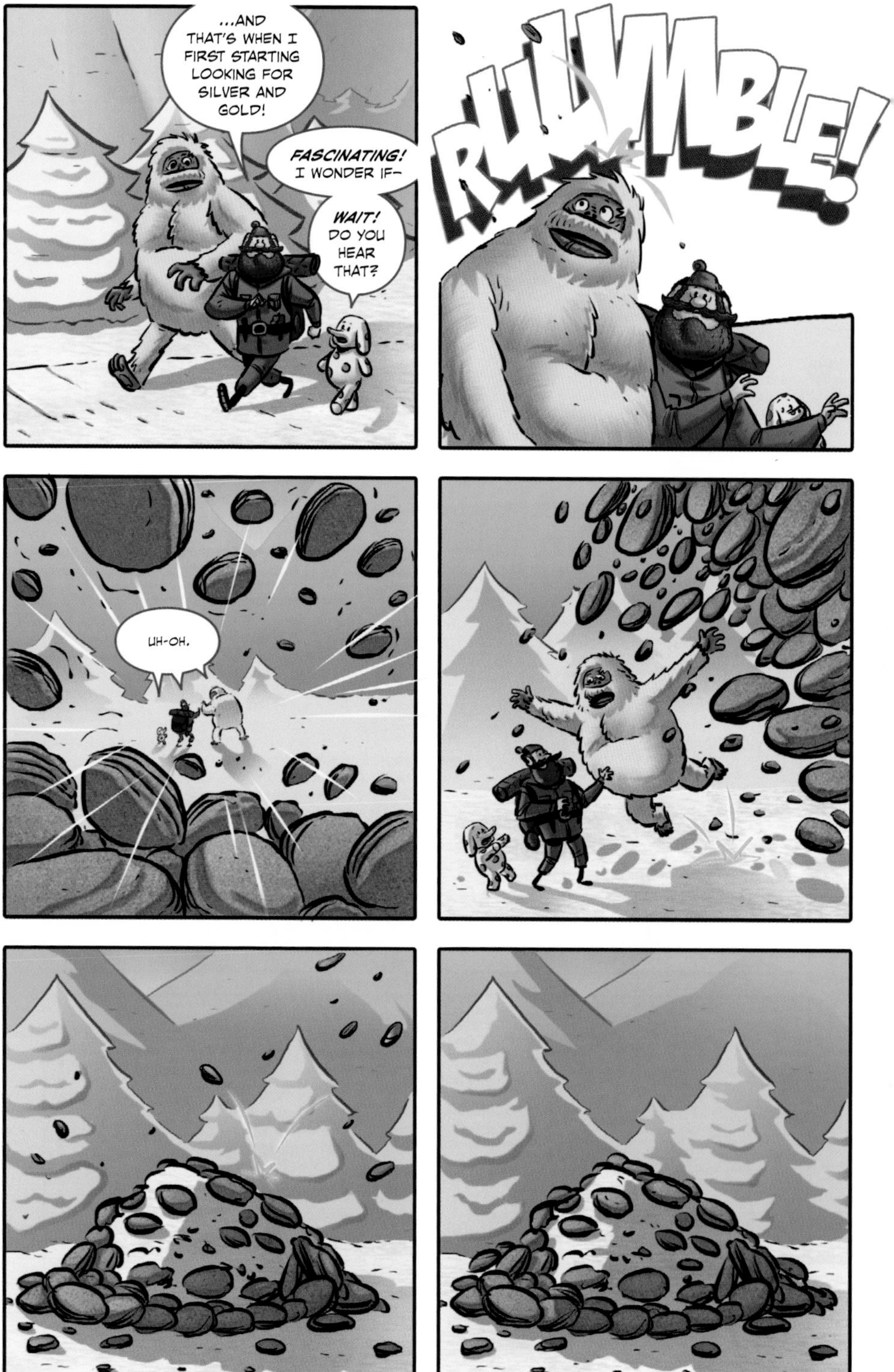
...AND THAT'S WHEN I FIRST STARTING LOOKING FOR SILVER AND GOLD!
FASCINATING! I WONDER IF–
WAIT! DO YOU HEAR THAT?
RRUMBLE!
UH-OH.

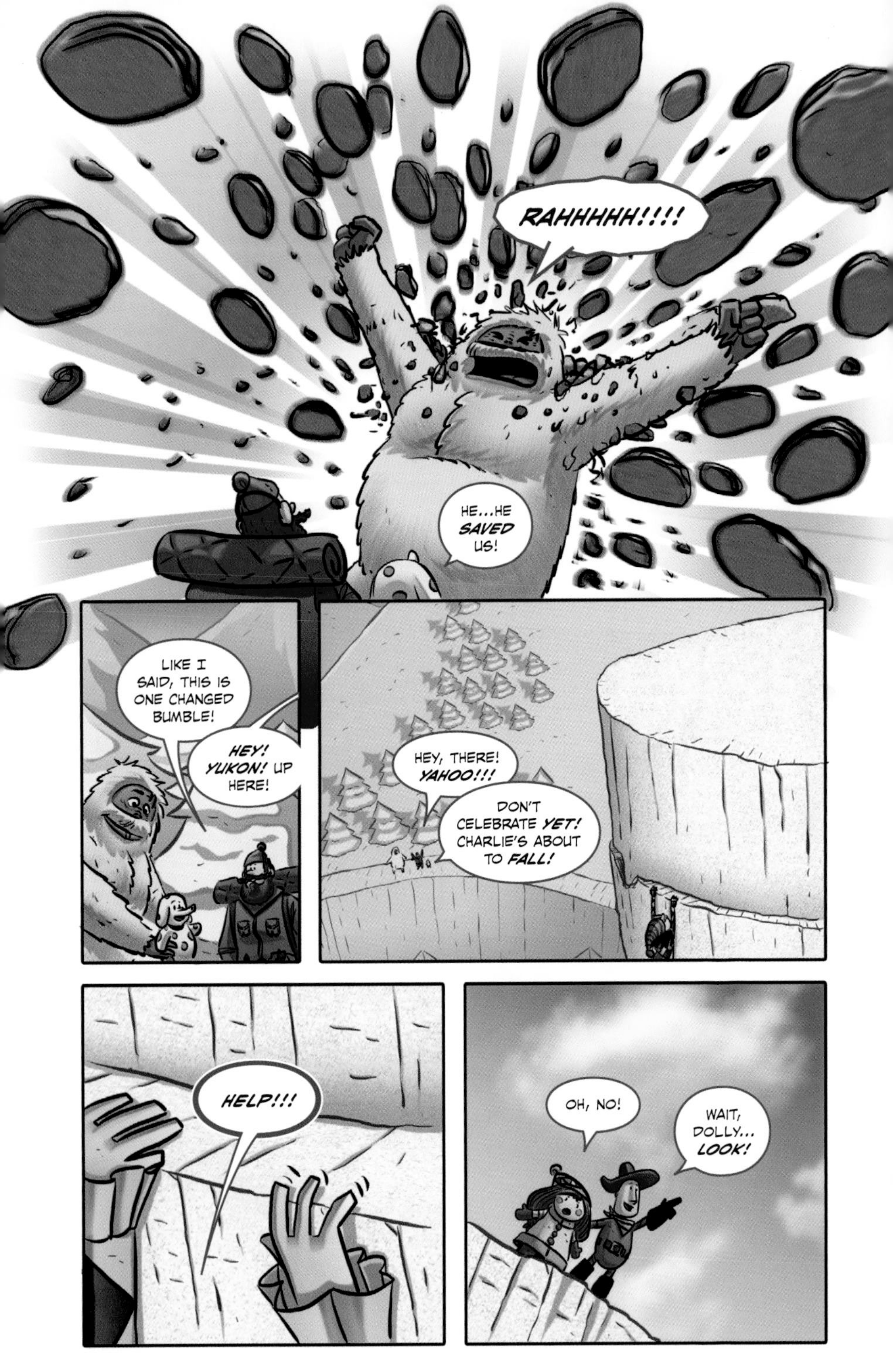
RAHHHHH!!!!
HE...HE SAVED US!
LIKE I SAID, THIS IS ONE CHANGED BUMBLE!
HEY! YUKON! UP HERE!
HEY, THERE! YAHOO!!!
DON'T CELEBRATE YET! CHARLIE'S ABOUT TO FALL!
HELP!!!
OH, NO!
WAIT, DOLLY... LOOK!

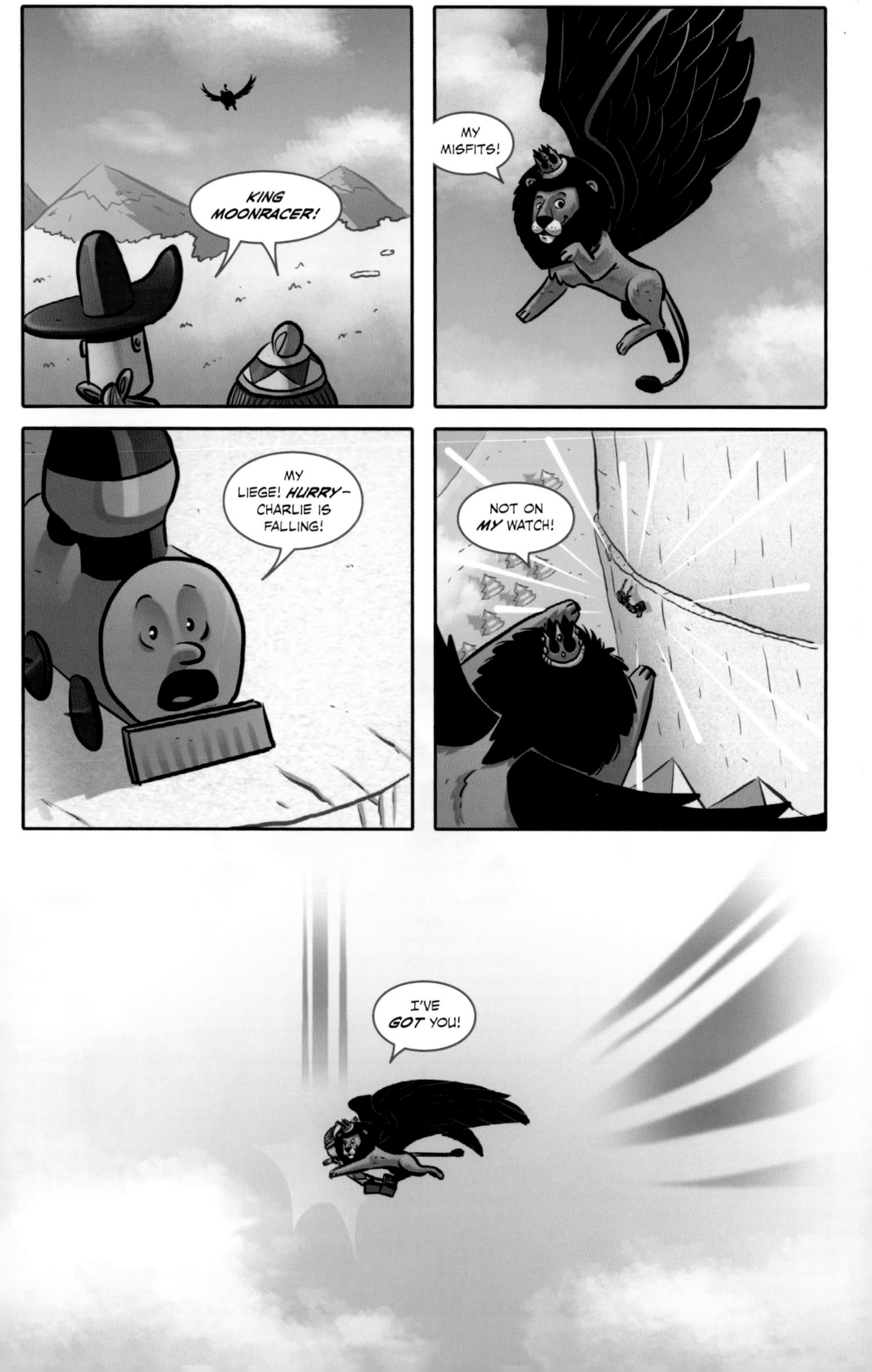
KING MOONRACER!
MY MISFITS!
MY LIEGE! HURRY— CHARLIE IS FALLING!
NOT ON MY WATCH!
I'VE GOT YOU!

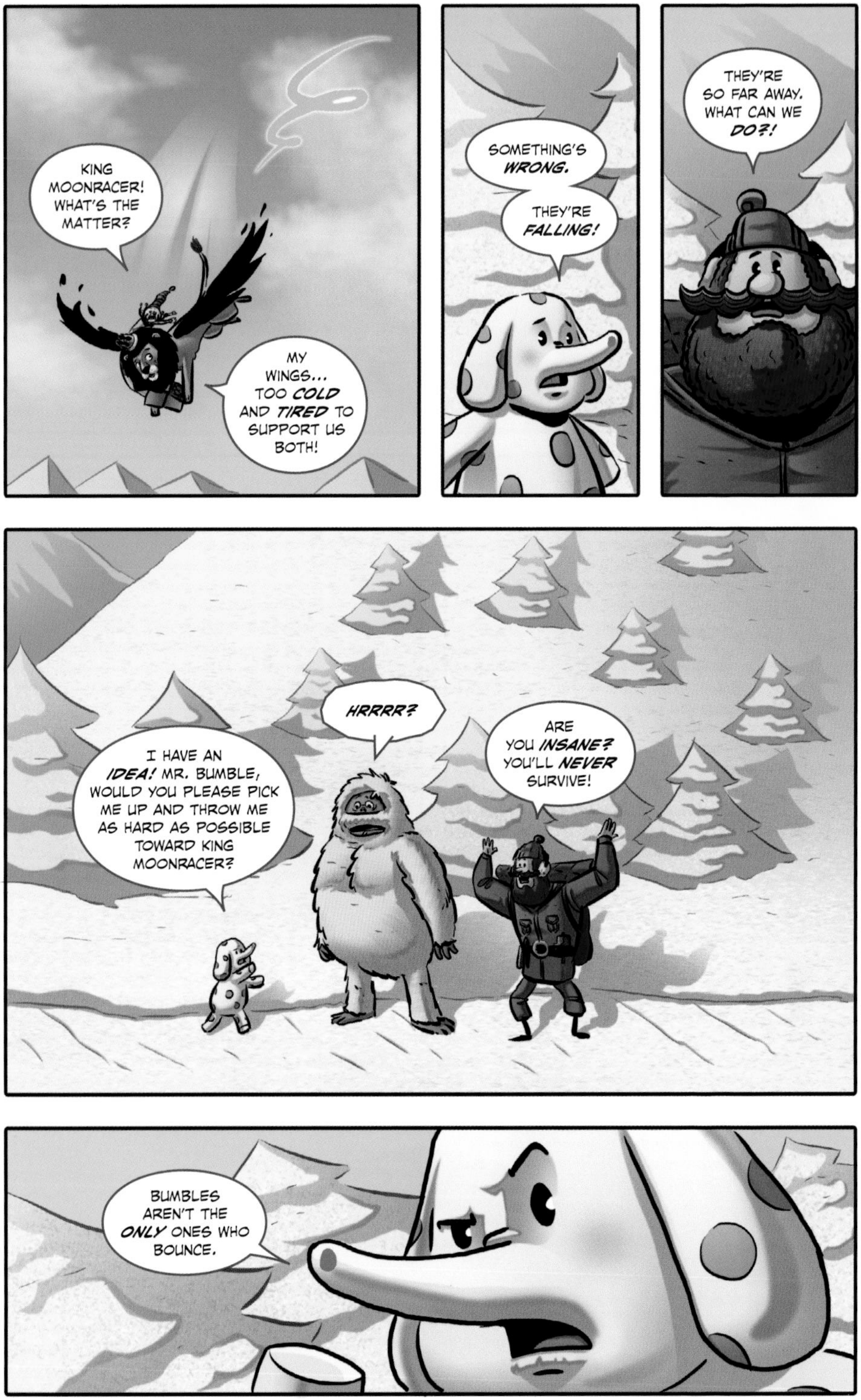

KING MOONRACER! WHAT'S THE MATTER?
MY WINGS... TOO COLD AND TIRED TO SUPPORT US BOTH!
SOMETHING'S WRONG.
THEY'RE FALLING!
THEY'RE SO FAR AWAY. WHAT CAN WE DO?!
I HAVE AN IDEA! MR. BUMBLE, WOULD YOU PLEASE PICK ME UP AND THROW ME AS HARD AS POSSIBLE TOWARD KING MOONRACER?
HRRRR?
ARE YOU INSANE? YOU'LL NEVER SURVIVE!
BUMBLES AREN'T THE ONLY ONES WHO BOUNCE.

HUH. THERE'S SOMETHING YOU DON'T SEE EVERY DAY.

GO, ELEPHANT! YOU CAN DO IT!

OOF!

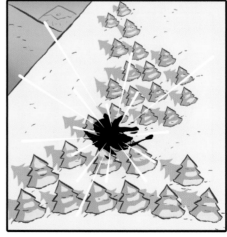

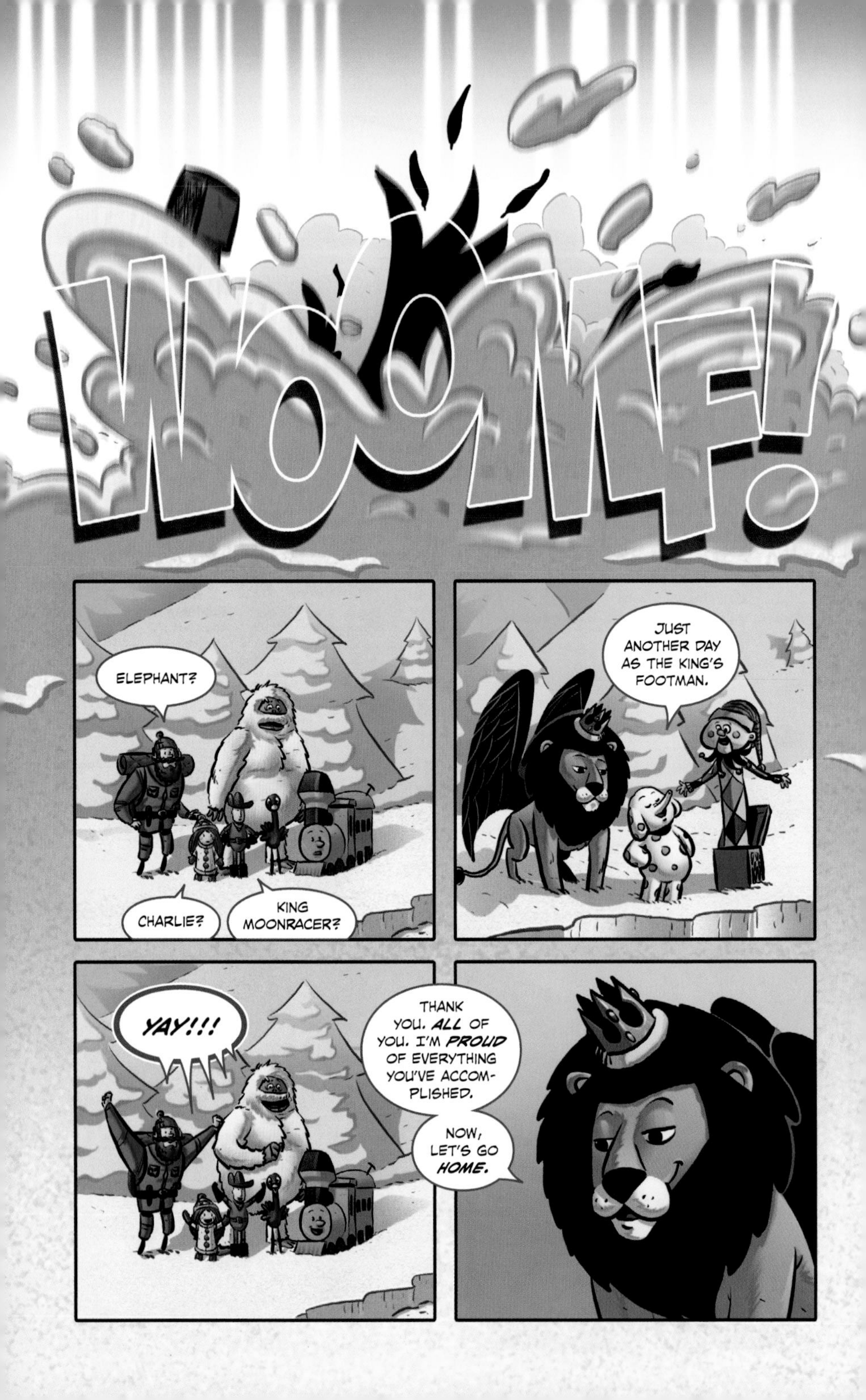
WOOMF!
ELEPHANT?
CHARLIE?
KING MOONRACER?
JUST ANOTHER DAY AS THE KING'S FOOTMAN.
YAY!!!
THANK YOU. ALL OF YOU. I'M PROUD OF EVERYTHING YOU'VE ACCOMPLISHED.
NOW, LET'S GO HOME.

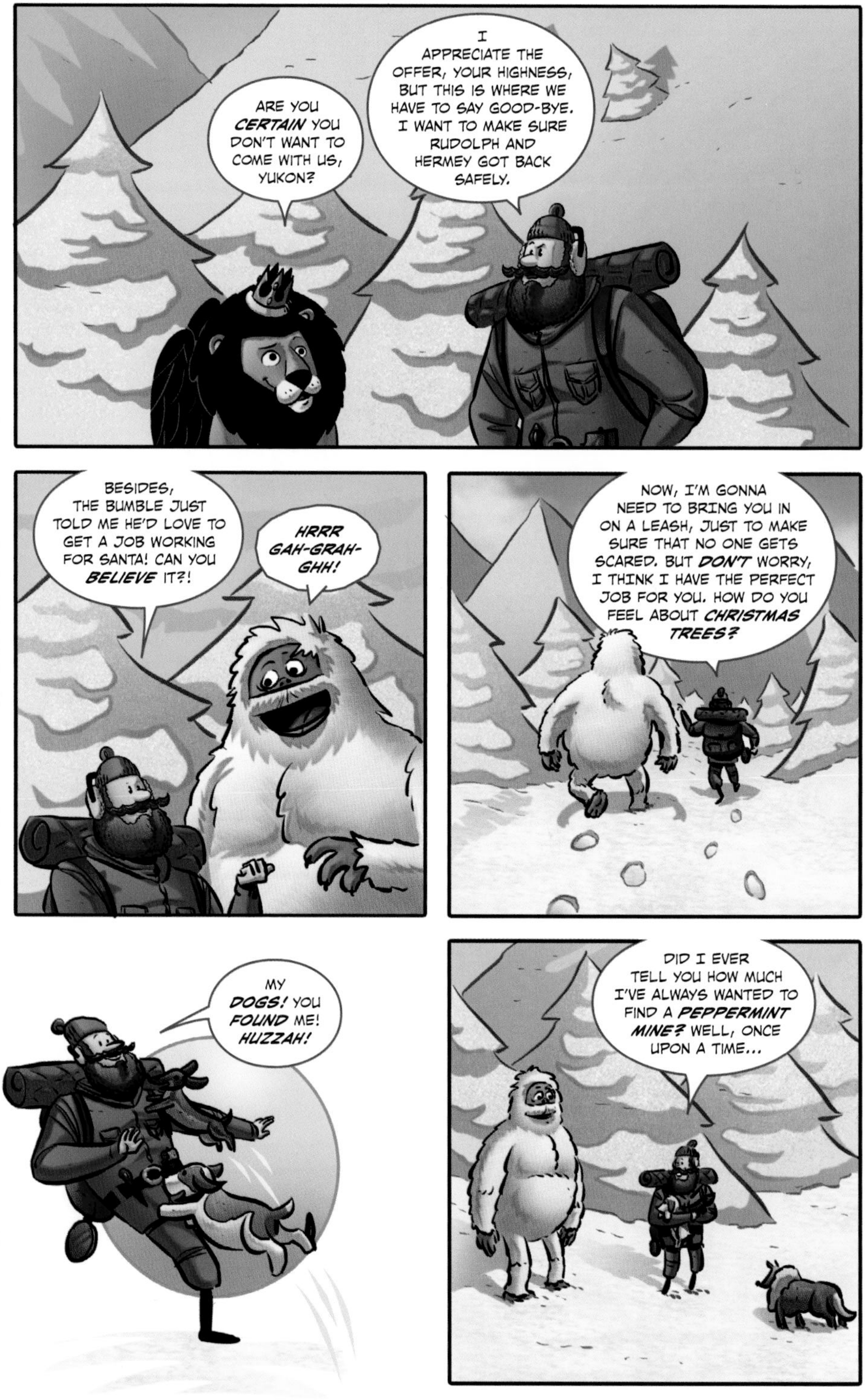
ARE YOU CERTAIN YOU DON'T WANT TO COME WITH US, YUKON?
I APPRECIATE THE OFFER, YOUR HIGHNESS, BUT THIS IS WHERE WE HAVE TO SAY GOOD-BYE. I WANT TO MAKE SURE RUDOLPH AND HERMEY GOT BACK SAFELY.
BESIDES, THE BUMBLE JUST TOLD ME HE'D LOVE TO GET A JOB WORKING FOR SANTA! CAN YOU BELIEVE IT?!
HRRR GAH-GRAH-GHH!
NOW, I'M GONNA NEED TO BRING YOU IN ON A LEASH, JUST TO MAKE SURE THAT NO ONE GETS SCARED. BUT DON'T WORRY, I THINK I HAVE THE PERFECT JOB FOR YOU. HOW DO YOU FEEL ABOUT CHRISTMAS TREES?
MY DOGS! YOU FOUND ME! HUZZAH!
DID I EVER TELL YOU HOW MUCH I'VE ALWAYS WANTED TO FIND A PEPPERMINT MINE? WELL, ONCE UPON A TIME...

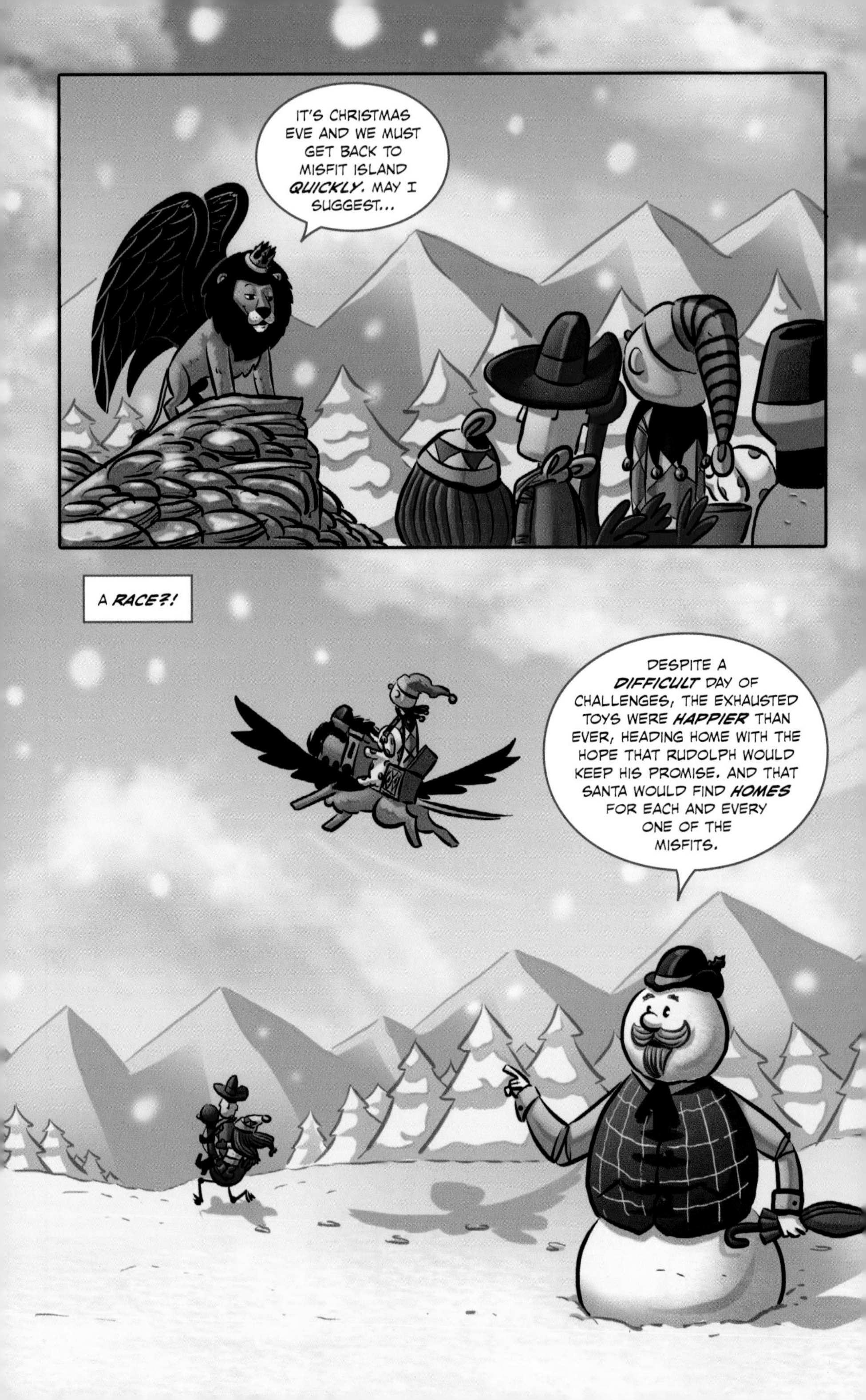
IT'S CHRISTMAS EVE AND WE MUST GET BACK TO MISFIT ISLAND QUICKLY. MAY I SUGGEST...
A RACE?!
DESPITE A DIFFICULT DAY OF CHALLENGES, THE EXHAUSTED TOYS WERE HAPPIER THAN EVER, HEADING HOME WITH THE HOPE THAT RUDOLPH WOULD KEEP HIS PROMISE. AND THAT SANTA WOULD FIND HOMES FOR EACH AND EVERY ONE OF THE MISFITS.

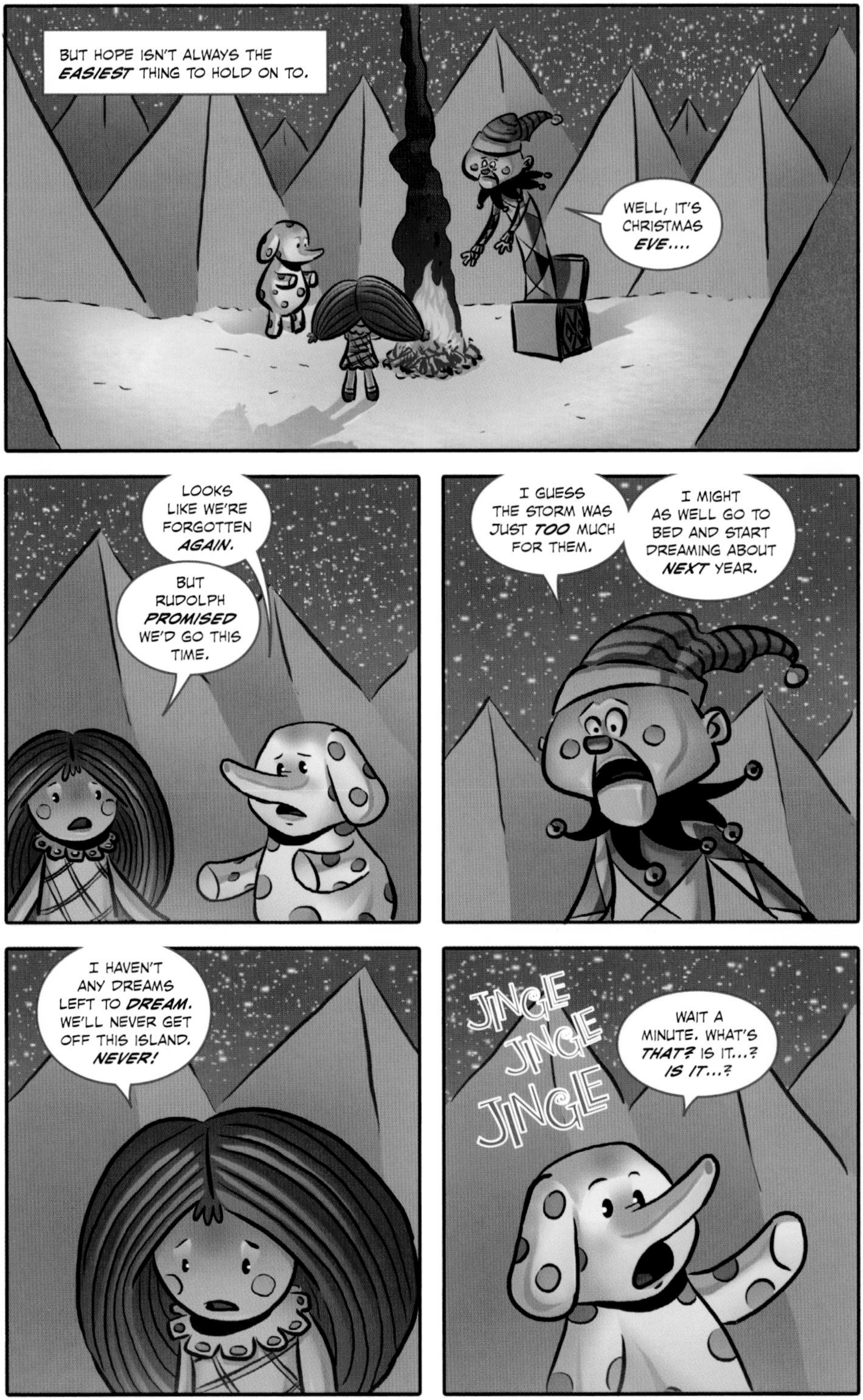
BUT HOPE ISN'T ALWAYS THE *EASIEST* THING TO HOLD ON TO.
WELL, IT'S CHRISTMAS *EVE*....
LOOKS LIKE WE'RE FORGOTTEN *AGAIN*.
BUT RUDOLPH *PROMISED* WE'D GO THIS TIME.
I GUESS THE STORM WAS JUST *TOO* MUCH FOR THEM.
I MIGHT AS WELL GO TO BED AND START DREAMING ABOUT *NEXT* YEAR.
I HAVEN'T ANY DREAMS LEFT TO *DREAM*. WE'LL NEVER GET OFF THIS ISLAND. *NEVER!*
JINGLE JINGLE JINGLE
WAIT A MINUTE. WHAT'S *THAT?* IS IT...? *IS IT...?*

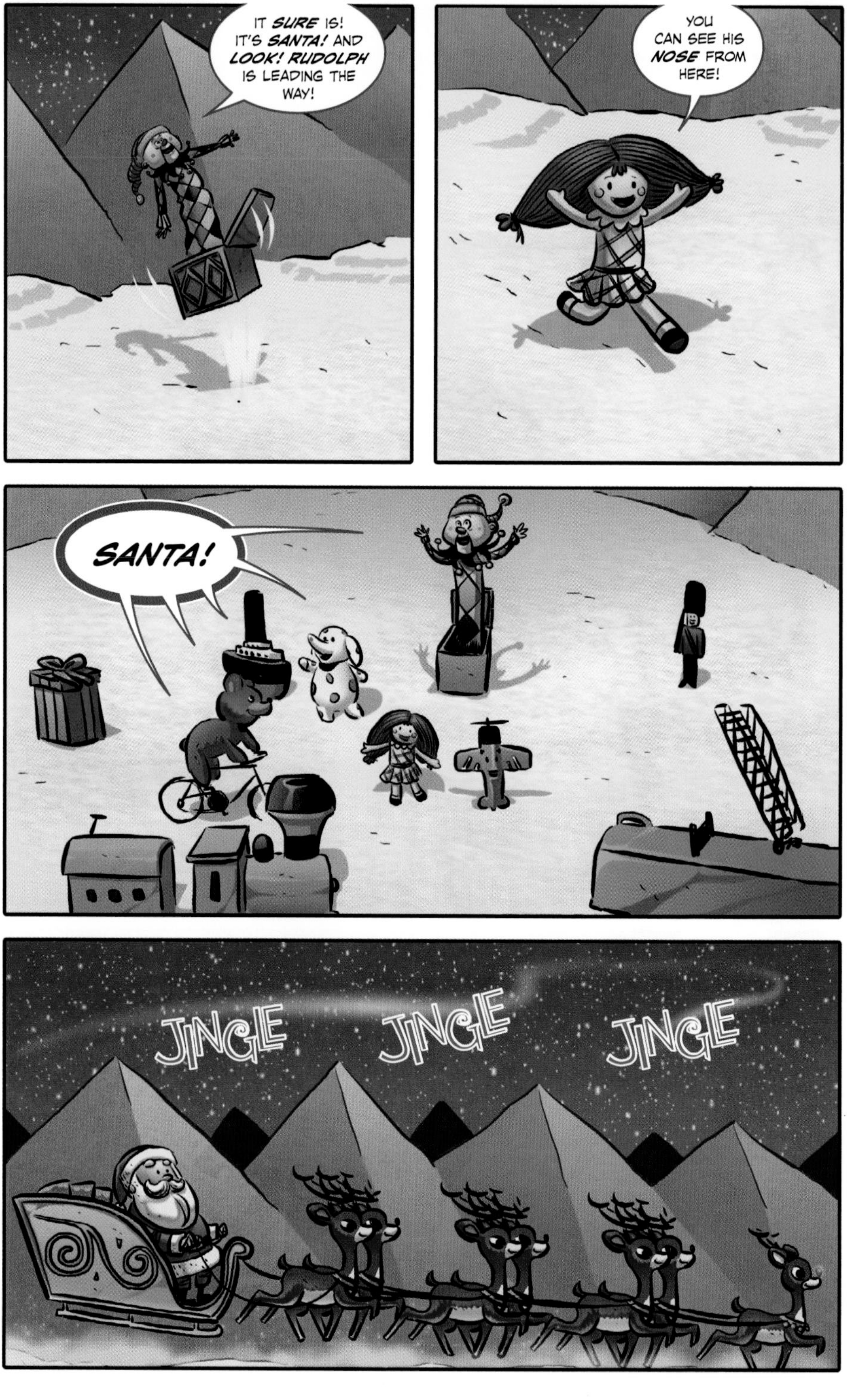
IT SURE IS! IT'S SANTA! AND LOOK! RUDOLPH IS LEADING THE WAY!
YOU CAN SEE HIS NOSE FROM HERE!
SANTA!
JINGLE
JINGLE
JINGLE

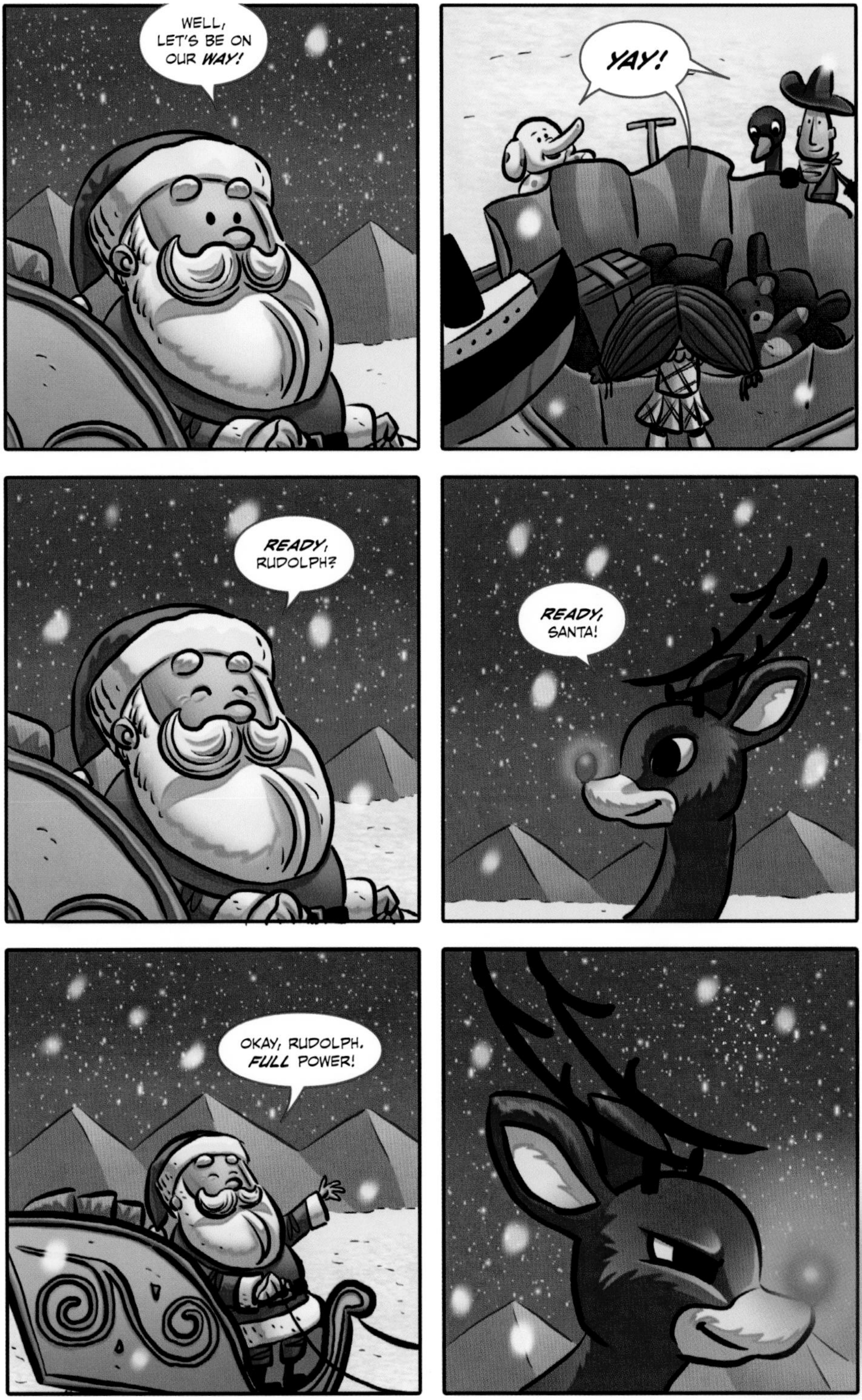
WELL, LET'S BE ON OUR WAY!
YAY!
READY, RUDOLPH?
READY, SANTA!
OKAY, RUDOLPH. FULL POWER!

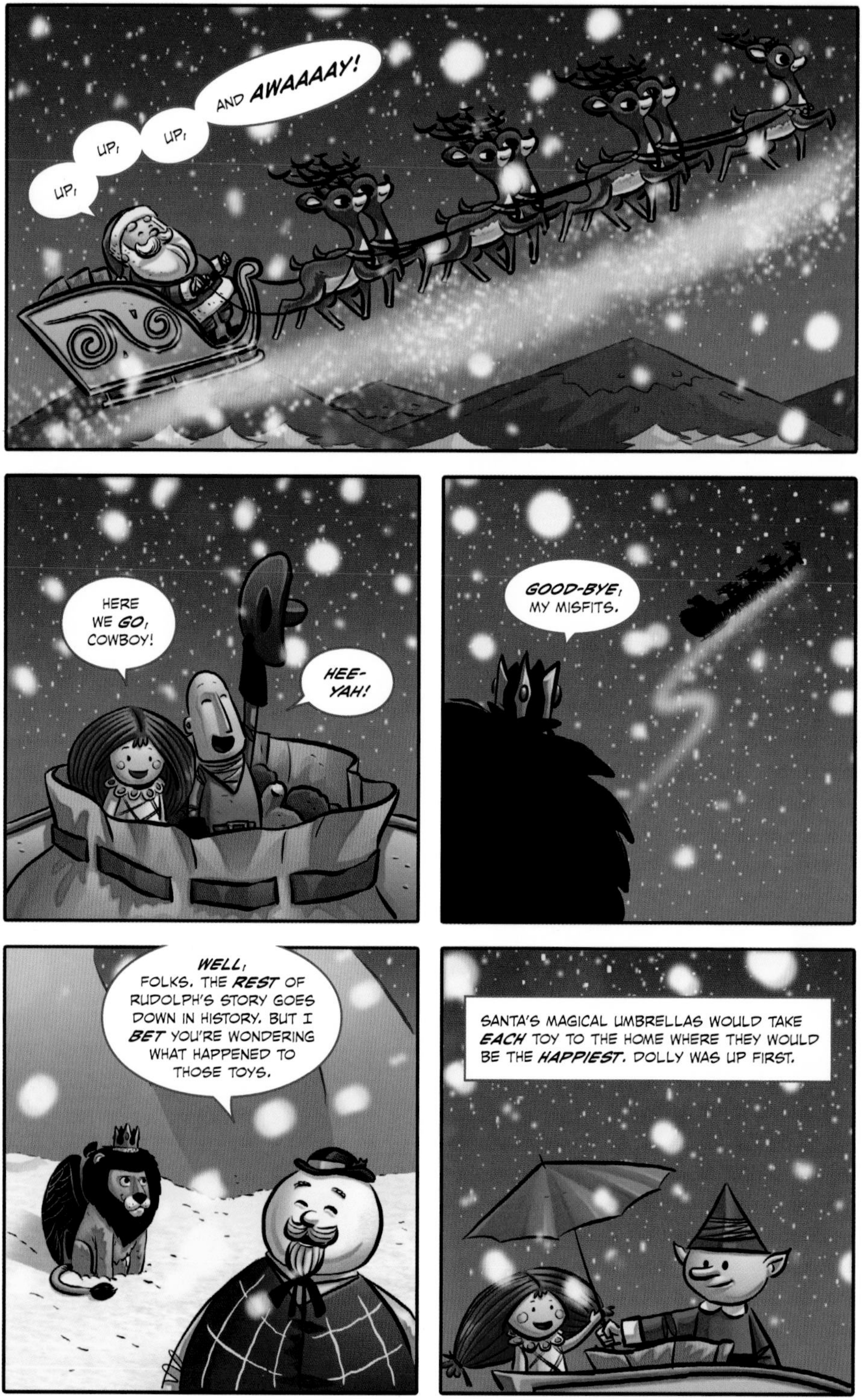
UP,
UP,
UP,
AND AWAAAAY!
HERE WE GO, COWBOY!
HEE-YAH!
GOOD-BYE, MY MISFITS.
WELL, FOLKS. THE REST OF RUDOLPH'S STORY GOES DOWN IN HISTORY. BUT I BET YOU'RE WONDERING WHAT HAPPENED TO THOSE TOYS.
SANTA'S MAGICAL UMBRELLAS WOULD TAKE EACH TOY TO THE HOME WHERE THEY WOULD BE THE HAPPIEST. DOLLY WAS UP FIRST.

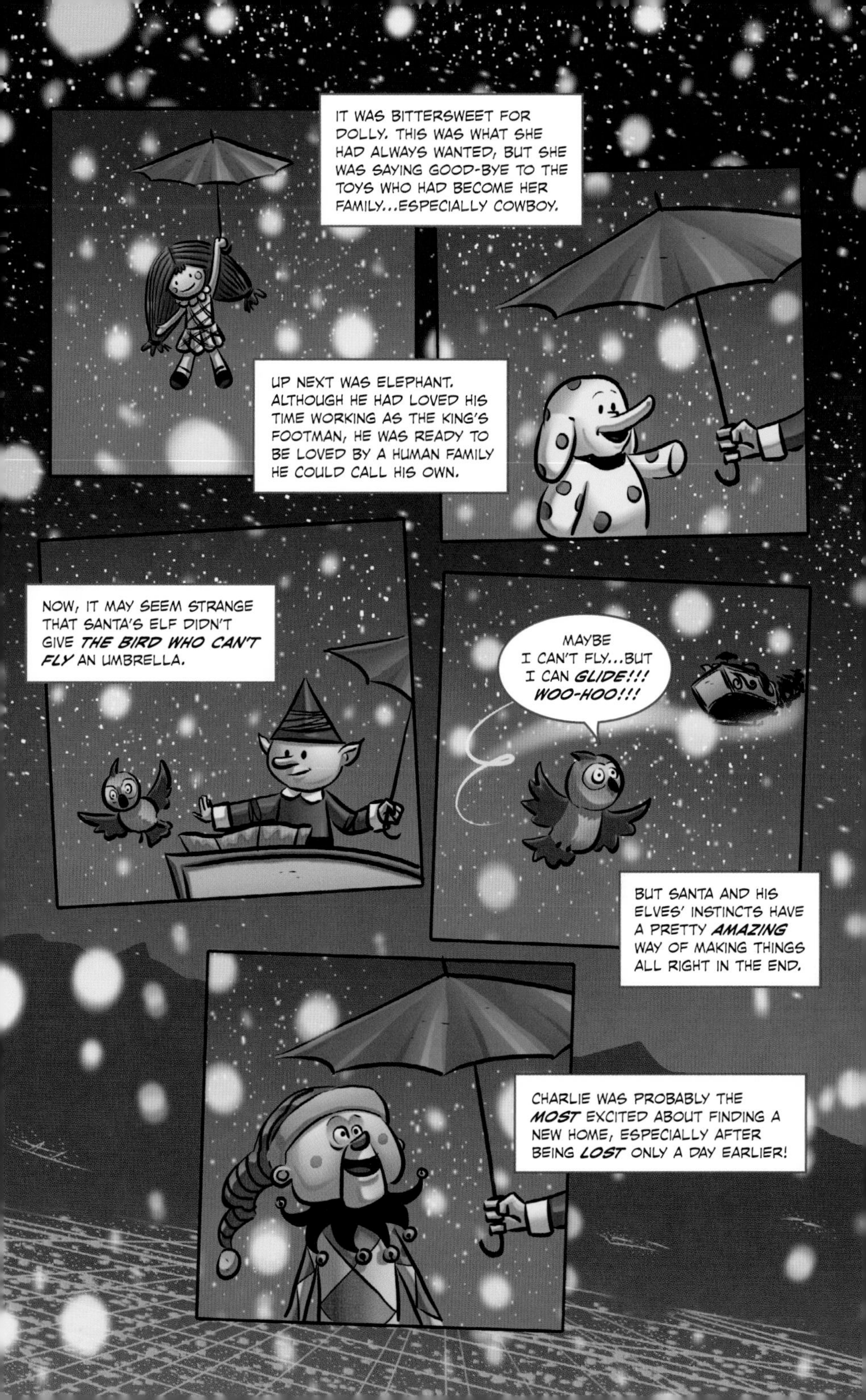
IT WAS BITTERSWEET FOR DOLLY. THIS WAS WHAT SHE HAD ALWAYS WANTED, BUT SHE WAS SAYING GOOD-BYE TO THE TOYS WHO HAD BECOME HER FAMILY...ESPECIALLY COWBOY.
UP NEXT WAS ELEPHANT. ALTHOUGH HE HAD LOVED HIS TIME WORKING AS THE KING'S FOOTMAN, HE WAS READY TO BE LOVED BY A HUMAN FAMILY HE COULD CALL HIS OWN.
NOW, IT MAY SEEM STRANGE THAT SANTA'S ELF DIDN'T GIVE ***THE BIRD WHO CAN'T FLY*** AN UMBRELLA.
MAYBE I CAN'T FLY...BUT I CAN ***GLIDE!!!*** ***WOO-HOO!!!***
BUT SANTA AND HIS ELVES' INSTINCTS HAVE A PRETTY ***AMAZING*** WAY OF MAKING THINGS ALL RIGHT IN THE END.
CHARLIE WAS PROBABLY THE ***MOST*** EXCITED ABOUT FINDING A NEW HOME, ESPECIALLY AFTER BEING ***LOST*** ONLY A DAY EARLIER!

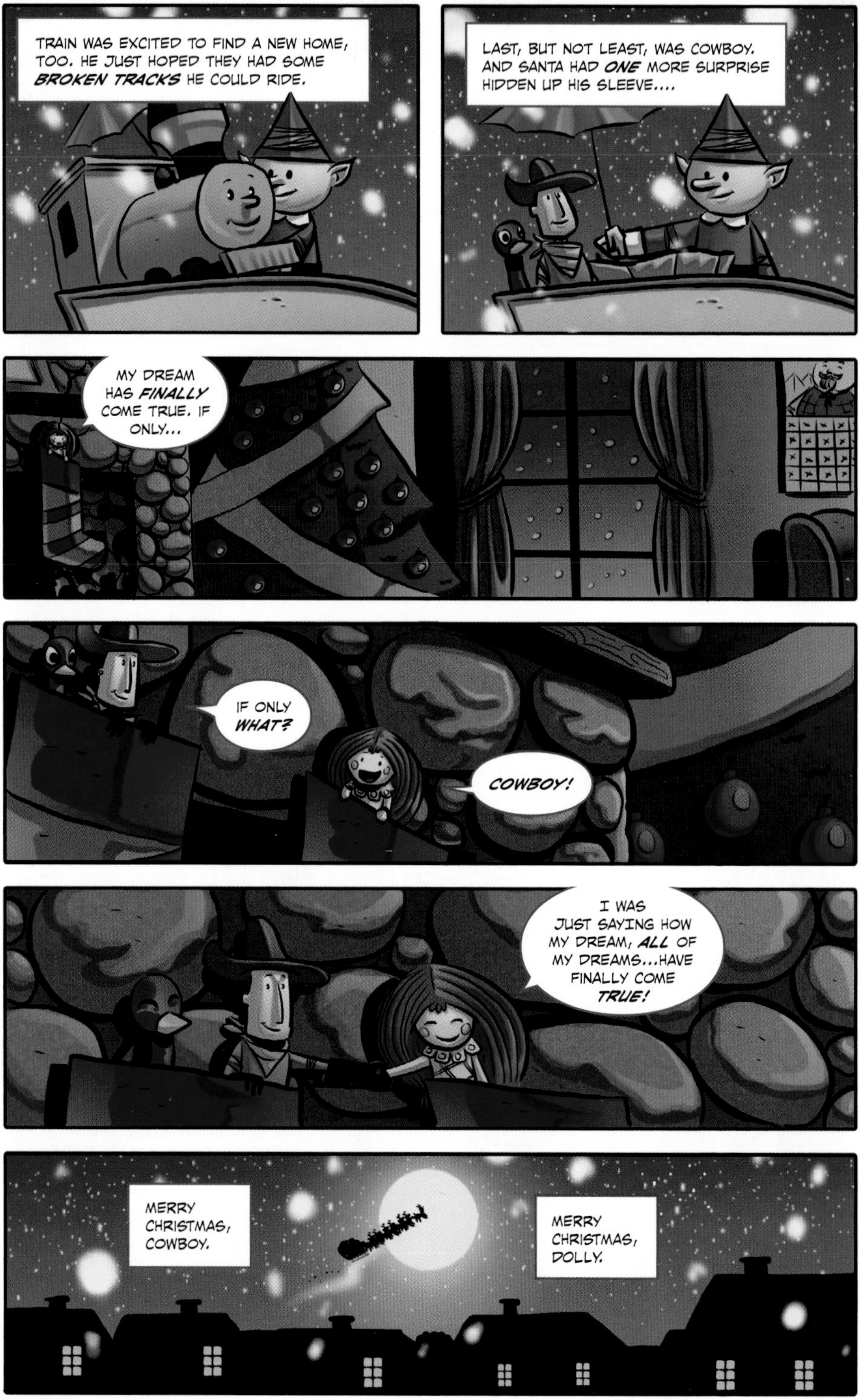
TRAIN WAS EXCITED TO FIND A NEW HOME, TOO. HE JUST HOPED THEY HAD SOME BROKEN TRACKS HE COULD RIDE.
LAST, BUT NOT LEAST, WAS COWBOY. AND SANTA HAD ONE MORE SURPRISE HIDDEN UP HIS SLEEVE....
MY DREAM HAS FINALLY COME TRUE. IF ONLY...
IF ONLY WHAT?
COWBOY!
I WAS JUST SAYING HOW MY DREAM, ALL OF MY DREAMS...HAVE FINALLY COME TRUE!
MERRY CHRISTMAS, COWBOY.
MERRY CHRISTMAS, DOLLY.

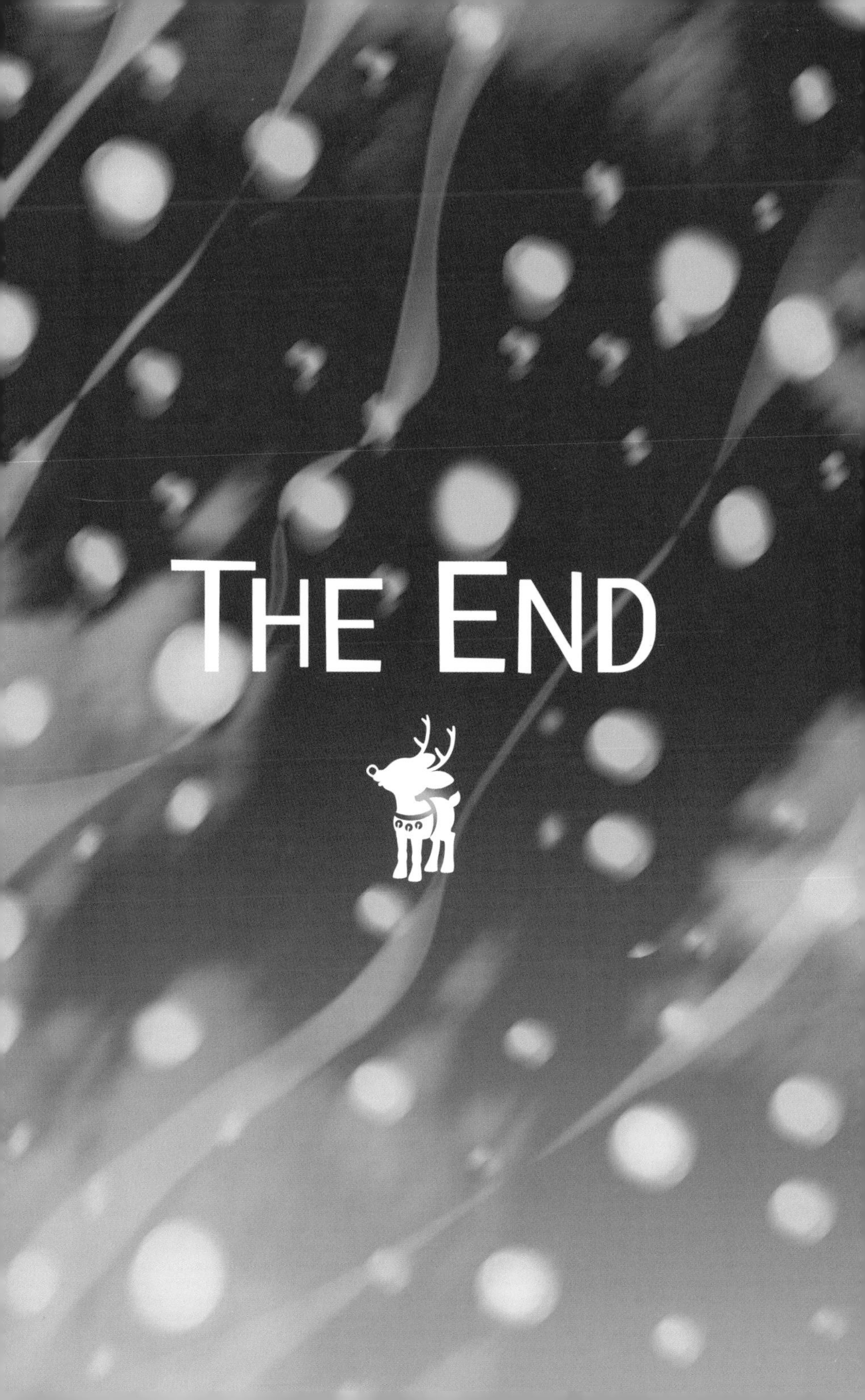
THE END